TED AND THE TELEPHONE

Also by Sara Ware Bassett

THE YOUNG ENGINEERS	**THE STORY OF**
Carl and the Cotton Gin	The Story of Glass
Christopher and the Clockmakers	The Story of Leather
Paul and the Printing Press	The Story of Silk
Steve and the Steam Engine	The Story of Sugar
Ted and the Telephone	The Story of Porcelain
Walter and the Wireless	The Story of Lumber
	The Story of Wool

This edition published 2026
by Living Book Press
Copyright © Living Book Press, 2026

ISBN: 978-1-76153-451-5 (hardcover)
         978-1-76153-453-9 (softcover)

First published in 1922.

This edition is based on the Little, Brown, and Company printing by 1922.

A catalogue record for this book is available from the National Library of Australia

TED AND THE TELEPHONE

by

SARA WARE BASSETT

"WOULD YOU LIKE TO GO TO COLLEGE IF YOU COULD?" PERSISTED THE ELDER MAN

Contents

EDWIN T. HOLMES
WHO PLAYED A PART IN THE WONDERFUL
TELEPHONE STORY, THIS
BOOK IS AFFECTIONATELY INSCRIBED.
                                        S. W. B.

CHAPTER I

AN UNHERALDED CHAMPION

Ted Turner lived at Freeman's Falls, a sleepy little town on the bank of a small New Hampshire river. There were cotton mills in the town; in fact, had there not been probably no town would have existed. The mills had not been attracted to the town; the town had arisen because of the mills. The river was responsible for the whole thing, for its swift current and foaming cascades had brought the mills, and the mills in turn had brought the village.

Ted's father was a shipping clerk in one of the factories and his two older sisters were employed there also. Some day Ted himself expected to enter the great brick buildings, as the boys of the town usually did, and work his way up. Perhaps in time he might become a superintendent or even one of the firm. Who could tell? Such miracles did happen. Not that Ted Turner preferred a life in the cotton mills to any other career. Not at all. Deep down in his soul he detested the humming, panting, noisy place with its clatter of wheels, its monotonous piecework, and its limited horizon. But what choice had he? The mills were there and the only alternative before him. It was the mills or nothing, for people seldom came to live at Freeman's Falls if they did not intend to enter the factories of Fernald and Company. It was Fernald and Company that had led his father to sell the tumble-down farm in Vermont and move with his family to New Hampshire.

"There is no money in farming," announced he, after the death of Ted's mother. "Suppose we pull up stakes and go to some mill town where we can all find work."

And therefore, without consideration for personal preferences, they had looked up mill towns and eventually settled on Freeman's Falls, not because they particularly liked its location but because labor was needed there. A very sad decision it was for Ted who had passionately loved the old farm on which he had been born, the half-blind gray horse, the few hens, and the lean Jersey cattle that his father asserted ate more than they were worth. To be cooped up in a manufacturing center after having had acres of open country to roam over was not an altogether joyous prospect. Would there be any chestnut, walnut, or apple trees at Freeman's Falls, he wondered.

Alas, the question was soon answered. Within the village there were almost no trees at all except a few sickly elms and maples whose foliage was pale for want of sunshine and grimy with smoke. In fact, there was not much of anything in the town save the long dingy factories that bordered the river; the group of cheap and gaudy shops on the main street; and rows upon rows of wooden houses, all identical in design, walling in the highway. It was not a spot where green things flourished. There was not room for anything to grow and if there had been the soot from the towering chimneys would soon have settled upon any venturesome leaf or flower and quickly shrivelled it beneath a cloak of cinders. Even the river was coated with a scum of oil and refuse that poured from the waste pipes of the factories into the stream and washed up along the shores which might otherwise have been fair and verdant.

Of course, if one could get far enough away there was beauty in plenty for in the outlying country stretched vistas of splendid pines, fields lush with ferns and flowers, and the unsullied span of the river, where in all its mountain-born purity it rushed gaily down toward the village. Here, well distant from the manufacturing atmosphere, were the homes of the Fernalds who owned the mills, the great estates of Mr. Lawrence Fernald and Mr. Clarence Fernald who every day rolled to their offices in giant limousines. Everybody in Freeman's Falls knew them by sight,—the big boss, as he was called, and his married son; and everybody thought how lucky they were to own the mills and take the money instead of doing the work. At least, that was what gossip said they did.

Unquestionably it was much nicer to live at Aldercliffe, the stately colonial mansion of Mr. Lawrence Fernald; or at Pine Lea, the home of Mr. Clarence Fernald, where sweeping lawns, bright awnings, gardens, conservatories, and flashing fountains made a wonderland of the place. Troupes of laughing guests seemed always to be going and coming at both houses and there were horses and motor-cars, tennis courts, a golf course, and canoes and launches moored at the edge of the river. Freeman's Falls was a very stupid spot when contrasted with all this jollity. It must be far pleasanter, too, when winter came to hurry off to New York for the holidays or to Florida or California, as Mr. Clarence Fernald frequently did.

With money enough to do whatever one pleased, how could a person help being happy? And yet there were those who declared that both Mr. Lawrence and Mr. Clarence Fernald would have bartered their fortunes to have had the crippled heir to the Fernald millions strong like other boys. Occasionally Ted had caught a glimpse of this Laurie Fernald, a fourteen-year-old lad with thin, colorless face and eyes that were haunting with sadness. In the village he passed as "the poor little chap" or as "poor Master Laurie" and the employees always doffed their caps to him because they pitied him. Whether one liked Mr. Fernald or Mr. Clarence or did not, every one united in being sorry for Mr. Laurie. Perhaps the invalid realized this; at any rate, he never failed to return the greetings accorded him with a smile so gentle and sweet that it became a pleasure in the day of whomsoever received it.

It was said at the factories that the reason the Fernalds went to New York and Florida and California was because of Mr. Laurie; that was the reason, too, why so many celebrated doctors kept coming to Pine Lea, and why both Mr. Fernald and Mr. Clarence were often so sharp and unreasonable. In fact, almost everything the Fernalds did or did not do, said or did not say, could be traced back to Mr. Laurie. From the moment the boy was born—nay, long before—both Mr. Lawrence Fernald for whom he was named, and his father, Mr. Clarence Fernald, had planned how he should inherit the great mills and carry on the business they had founded. For years they had talked and talked of what should happen when Mr. Laurie grew up. And then had come the sudden and terrible illness, and after weeks of anxiety everybody realized that if Mr. Laurie lived he would be fortunate, and that he would never be able to carry on any business at all.

In what hushed tones the townspeople talked of the tragedy and how they speculated on what the Fernalds would do *now*. And how surprised the superintendent of one of the mills (who, by the way, had six husky boys of his own) had been to have Mr. Lawrence Fernald bridle with rage when he said he was sorry for him. A proud old man was Mr. Fernald, senior. He did not fancy being pitied, as his employees soon found out. Possibly Mr. Clarence Fernald did not like it any better but whether he did or not he at least had the courtesy not to show his feelings.

Thus the years had passed and Mr. Laurie had grown from childhood to boyhood. He could now ride about in a motorcar if lifted into it; but he could still walk very little, although specialists had not given up hope that perhaps in time he might be able to do so. There was a rumor that he was strapped into a steel jacket which he was forced to wear continually, and the mill hands commented on its probable discomfort and wondered how the boy could always keep so even-tempered. For it was unavoidable that the large force of servants from Aldercliffe and Pine Lea should neighbor back and forth with the townsfolk and in this way many a tale of Mr. Laurie's rare disposition reached the village. And even had not these stories been rife, anybody could easily have guessed the patience and sweetness of Mr. Laurie's nature from his smile.

Among the employees of Fernald and Company he was popularly known as the Little Master and between him and them there existed a friendliness which neither his father nor his grandfather had ever been able to call out. The difference was that for Mr. Lawrence Fernald the men did only what they were paid to do; for Mr. Clarence they did fully what they were paid to do; and for Mr. Laurie they would gladly have done what they were paid to do and a great deal more.

"The poor lad!" they murmured one to another. "The poor little chap!"

Of course it followed that no one envied Mr. Laurie his wealth. How could they? One might perhaps envy Mr. Fernald, senior, or Mr. Clarence; but never Mr. Laurie even though the Fernald fortune and all the houses and gardens, with their miles of acreage, as well as the vast cotton mills would one day be his. Even Ted Turner, poor as he was, and having only the prospect of the factories ahead of him, never thought of wishing to exchange his lot in life for that of Mr. Laurie. He would rather toil for Fernald and Company to his dying day than be this weak, dependent creature who was compelled to be carried about by those stronger than himself.

Nevertheless, in spite of this, there were intervals when Ted did wish he might exchange houses with Mr. Laurie. Not that Ted Turner coveted the big colonial mansion, or its fountains, its pergolas, its wide lawns; but he did love gardens, flowers, trees, and sky, and of these he had very little. He was, to be sure, fortunate in living on the outskirts of the village where he had more green and blue than did most of the mill workers. Still, it was not like Vermont and the unfenced miles of country to which he had been accustomed. A small tenement in Freeman's Falls, even though it had steam heat and running water, was in his opinion a poor substitute for all that had been left behind.

But Ted's father liked the new home better, far better, and so did Ruth and Nancy, his sisters. Many a time the boy heard his father congratulating himself that he was clear of the farm and no longer had to get up in the cold of the early morning to feed and water the stock and do the milking. And Ruth and Nancy echoed these felicitations and rejoiced that now there was neither butter to churn nor hens to care for.

Even Ted was forced to confess that Freeman's Falls had its advantages. Certainly the school was better, and as his father had resolved to keep him in it at least a part of the high-school term, Ted felt himself to be a lucky boy. He liked to study. He did not like all studies, of course. For example, he detested Latin, French, and history; but he revelled in shop-work, math-

"You can't be spreadin' wires an' jars an' things round my room!" protested Mr. Turner.

ematics, and the sciences. There was nothing more to his taste than putting things together, especially electrical things; and already he had tried at home several crude experiments with improvised telegraphs, telephones, and wireless contrivances. Doubtless he would have had many more such playthings had not materials cost so much, money been so scarce, and Ruth and Nancy so timid. They did not like mysterious sparks and buzzings in the pantry and about the kitchen and told him so in no uncertain terms.

"The next thing you know you'll be setting the house afire!" Ruth had asserted. "Besides, we've no room for wires and truck around here. You'll have to take your clutter somewhere else."

And so Ted had obediently bundled his precious possessions into the room where he slept with his father only to be as promptly ejected from that refuge also.

"You can't be spreadin' wires an' jars an' things round my room!" protested Mr. Turner with annoyance.

It did not seem to occur to him that it was Ted's room as well,—the only room the boy had.

Altogether, his treasures found no welcome anywhere in the tiny apartment, and at length convinced of this, Ted took everything down and stowed it away in a box beneath the bed, henceforth confining his scientific adventures to the school laboratories where they might possibly have remained forever but for Mr. Wharton, the manager of the farms at Aldercliffe and Pine Lea.

CHAPTER II

TED RENEWS OLD TIMES

Mr. Wharton was about the last person on earth one would have connected with boxes of strings and wires hidden away beneath beds. He was a graduate of a Massachusetts agricultural college; a keen-eyed, quick, impatient creature toward whom people in general stood somewhat in awe. He had the reputation of being a top-notch farmer and those who knew him declared with zest that there was nothing he did not know about soils, fertilizers, and crops. There was no nonsense when Mr. Wharton appeared on the scene. The men who worked for him soon found that out. You didn't lean on your hoe, light your pipe, and hazard the guess that there would be rain to-morrow; you just hoed as hard as you could and did not stop to guess anything.

Now it happened that it was haying time both at Aldercliffe and Pine Lea and the rumor got abroad that the crop was an unusually heavy one; that Mr. Wharton was short of help and ready to hire at a good wage extra men from the adjoining village. Mr. Turner brought the tidings home from the mill one June night when he returned from work.

"Why don't you try for a job up at Aldercliffe, my lad?" concluded he, after stating the case. "Ever since you were knee-high to a grasshopper you had a knack for pitching hay. Besides, you'd make a fine bit of money and the work would be no heavier than handling freight down at the mills. You've got to work somewhere through your summer vacation."

He made the latter statement as a matter of course for a matter of course it had long since become. Ted always worked when he was not studying. Vacations, holidays, Saturdays, he was always busy earning money for if he had not been, there would have been no chance of his going to school the rest of the time. Sometimes he did errands for one of the dry-goods stores; sometimes, if there were a vacancy, he helped in Fernald and Company's shipping rooms; sometimes he worked at the town market or rode about on the grocer's wagon, delivering orders. By one means or another he had usually contrived, since he was quite a small boy, to pick up odd sums that went toward his clothes and "keep." As he grew older, these sums had increased until now they had become a recognized part of the family income. For it was understood that Ted would turn in toward the household expenses all that he earned. His father had never believed in a boy having money to spend and even if he had, every cent which the Turners could scrape together was needed at home. Ted knew well how much sugar and butter cost and therefore without demur he cheerfully placed in the hands of his sister Ruth, who ran the house, every farthing that was given him.

From childhood this sense of responsibility had always been in his background. He had known what it was to go hungry that he might have shoes and go without shoes that he might have underwear. Money had been very scarce on the Vermont farm, and although there was now more of it than there ever had been in the past, nevertheless it was not plentiful. Therefore, as vacation was approaching and he must get a job anyway, he decided to present himself before Mr. Wharton and ask for a chance to help in harvesting the hay crops at Aldercliffe and Pine Lea.

"You are younger than the men I am hiring," Mr. Wharton said, after he had scanned the lad critically. "How old are you?"

"Fourteen."

"I thought as much. What I want is men."

"But I have farmed all my life," protested Ted with spirit.

"Indeed!" the manager exclaimed not unkindly. "Where?"

"In Vermont."

"You don't say so! I was born in the Green Mountains," was the quick retort. "Where did you live?"

"Newfane."

Instantly the man's face lighted.

"I know that place well. And you came from Newfane here? How did you happen to do that?"

"My father could not make the farm pay and we needed money."

"Humph! Were you sorry to give up farming?"

"Yes, sir. I didn't want to come to Freeman's Falls. But," added the boy brightening, "I like the school here."

The manager paused, studying the sharp, eager face, the spare figure, and the fine carriage of the lad before him.

"Do you like haying?" asked he presently.

"Not particularly," Ted owned with honesty.

Mr. Wharton laughed.

"I see you are a human boy," he said. "If you don't like it, why are you so anxious to do it now?"

"I've got to earn some money or give up going to school in the fall."

"Oh, so that's it! And what are you working at in school that is so alluring?" demanded the man with a quizzical glance.

"Electricity."

"Electricity!"

"Wireless, telegraphs, telephones, and things like that," put in Ted.

For comment Mr. Wharton tipped back in his chair and once more let his eye wander over the boy's face; then he wheeled abruptly around to his desk, opened a drawer, and took out a yellow card across which he scrawled a line with his fountain pen.

"You may begin work to-morrow morning," he remarked curtly. "If it is pleasant, Stevens will be cutting the further meadow with a gang of men. Come promptly at eight o'clock, prepared to stay all day, and bring this card with you."

He waved the bit of pasteboard to and fro in the air an instant to be certain that the ink on it was dry and afterward handed it to Ted. Instinctively the boy's gaze dropped to the message written upon it and before he realized it he had read the brief words:

"Ted Turner. He says he has farmed in Vermont. If he shows any evidence of it keep him. If not turn him off. Wharton."

The man in the chair watched him as he read.

"Well?" said he.

"I beg your pardon, sir. I did not mean to read it," Ted replied with a start. "I'm very much obliged to you for giving me the job."

"I don't see that you've got it yet."

"But I shall have," asserted the lad confidently. "All I asked was a chance."

"That's all the world gives any of us," responded the manager gruffly, as he drew forth a sheet of paper and began to write. "Nobody can develop our brains, train our muscles, or save our souls but ourselves."

With this terse observation he turned his back on the boy, and after loitering a moment to make sure that he had nothing more to say, the lad slipped away, triumphantly bearing with him the coveted morsel of yellow pasteboard. That its import was noncommittal and even contained a tang of skepticism troubled him not a whit. The chief thing was that he had wrested from the manager an opportunity, no matter how grudgingly accorded, to show what he was worth. He could farm and he knew it and he had no doubt that he could demonstrate the fact to any boss he might encounter.

Therefore with high courage he was promptly on hand the next morning and even before the time assigned he approached Stevens, the superintendent.

"What do you want, youngster?" demanded the man sharply. He was in a hurry and it was obvious that something had nettled him and that he was in no humor to be delayed.

"I came to help with the haying."

"We don't want any boys as young as you," Stevens returned, moving away.

"I've a card from Mr. Wharton."

"A card, eh? Why didn't you say so in the first place? Shell it out."

Shyly Ted produced his magic fragment of paper which the overseer read with disapproval in his glance.

"Well, since Wharton wants you tried out, you can pitch in with the crowd," grumbled he. "But I still think you're too young. I've had boys your age before and never found them any earthly use. However, you won't be here long if you're not—that's one thing. You'll find a pitchfork in the barn. Follow along behind the men who are mowing and spread the grass out."

"I know."

"Oh, you do, do you! Trust people your size for knowing everything."

To the final remark the lad vouchsafed no reply. Instead he moved away and soon returned, fork in hand. What a flood of old memories came surging back with the touch of the implement! Again he was in Vermont in the stretch of mowings that fronted the old white house where he was born. The scent of the hay in his nostrils stirred him like an elixir, and with a thrill of pleasure he set to work. He had not anticipated toiling out there in the hot sunshine at a task which he had always disliked; but to-day, by a strange miracle, it did not seem to be a task so much as a privilege.

How familiar the scene was! As he approached the group of older men it took him only a second to see where he was needed and he thrust his pitchfork into the swath at his feet with a swing of easy grace.

"Guess you've done this job before," called a man behind him after he had worked for an interval.

"Yes, I have."

"You show it," was the brief observation.

They moved on in silence up the field.

"Where'd you learn to handle that fork, sonny?" another voice shouted, as they neared the farther wall.

"In Vermont," laughed Ted.

"I judged as much," grunted the speaker. "They don't train up farmers of your size in this part of the world."

Ted flushed with pleasure and for the first time he stopped work and mopped the perspiration from his forehead. He was hot and thirsty but he found himself strangely exhilarated by the exercise and the sweet morning air and sunshine. Again he took up his fork and tossed the newly cut grass up into the light, spreading it on the ground with a methodical sweep of his young arm. The sun had risen higher now and its dazzling brilliance poured all about him. Up and down the meadow he went and presently he was surprised to find himself alone near the point from which he had started. His fellow-laborers were no longer in sight. The field was very still and because it was, Ted began to whistle softly to himself.

He was startled to hear a quiet laugh at his elbow.

"Don't you ever eat anything, kid?"

Mr. Wharton was standing beside him, a flicker of amusement in his gray eyes.

"I didn't know it was noon," gasped Ted.

"We'll have to tie an alarm clock on you," chuckled the manager. "The gang stopped work a quarter of an hour ago."

"I didn't notice they had."

The boy flushed. He felt very foolish to have been discovered working there all by himself in this ridiculous fashion.

"I wanted to finish this side of the field and I forgot about the time," he stammered apologetically.

"Have you done it to your satisfaction?"

"Yes, I'm just through."

For the life of him Ted could not tell whether the manager was laughing at him or not. He kicked the turf sheepishly.

"Aren't you tired?" inquired Mr. Wharton at length.

"No—at least—well, I haven't thought about it. Perhaps I am a little."

"And well you may be. You've put in a stiff morning's work. You'd better go and wash up now and eat your lunch. Take your full hour of rest. No matter if the others do get back here before you. Stevens says you are worth any two of them, anyway."

"It's just that I'm used to it," was the modest reply.

"We'll let it go at that," Mr. Wharton returned ambiguously. "And one thing more before you go. You needn't worry about staying on. We can use you one way or another all summer. There'll always be work for a boy who knows how to do a job well."

CHAPTER III

GOING TO HOUSEKEEPING

Thus it came about that Ted Turner began the long, golden days of his summer vacation at the great estates of the Fernalds, and soon he had made himself such an indispensable part of the farming staff that both Mr. Wharton and Mr. Stevens came to rely on him for many services outside of those usually turned over to the men.

"Just step over to the south lot at Pine Lea, Ted, and see if those fellows are thinning the beets properly," Mr. Wharton would say. "I gave them their orders but they may not have taken them in. You know how the thing should be done. Sing out to them if they are not doing the job right."

Or:

"Mr. Stevens and I shall be busy this morning checking up the pay roll. Suppose you have an eye on the hilling up of the potatoes, Ted. Show the men how you want it done and start them at it. I'll be over later to see how it's going."

Frequently, instead of working, the boy was called in to give an opinion on some agricultural matter with which he had had experience.

"We are finding white grubs in the corner of the Pine Lea garden. They are gnawing off the roots of the plants and making no end of trouble. What did you do to get rid of them when you were up in Vermont?"

"Salt and wood ashes worked better than anything else," Ted would reply modestly. "It might not be any good here but we had luck with it at home."

"We can try it, at least. You tell Mr. Stevens what the proportions are and how you applied it."

And because the advice was followed by a successful extermination of the plague, the lad's prestige increased and he was summoned to future conclaves when troublesome conditions arose.

Now and then there was a morning when Mr. Stevens would remark to Mr. Wharton:

"I've got to go to the Falls to-day to see about some freight. Ted Turner will be round here, though, and I guess things will be all right. The men can ask him if they want anything."

And so it went.

First Ted filled one corner, then another. He did errands for Mr. Wharton, very special errands, that required thought and care, and which the manager would not have entrusted to every one. Sometimes he ventured valuable suggestions which Mr. Stevens, who really had had far less farming experience than he, was only too grateful to follow.

If the boy felt at all puffed up by the dependence placed upon him, he certainly failed to show it. On the contrary he did his part enthusiastically, faithfully, generously, and without a thought of praise or reward. Although he was young to direct others, when he did give orders to the men he was tactful and retiring enough to issue his commands in the form of wishes and immediately they were heeded without protest. He never shirked the hard work he asked others to perform but was always ready to roll up the sleeves of his blue jeans and pitch with vigor into any task, no matter how menial it was. Had he been arrogant and made an overbearing use of his authority, the men would quickly have rated him as a conceited little popinjay, the pet of the boss, and made his life miserable; but as he remained quite unspoiled by the preference shown him and exhibited toward every one he encountered a kindly sympathy and consideration, the workmen soon accepted him as a matter of course and even began to turn to him whenever a dilemma confronted them.

Perhaps Ted was too genuinely interested in what he was doing to think much about himself or realize that the place he held was an unusual one. At home he and his father had threshed out many a problem together and each given to it the best his brain had to offer, without thought of the difference in their ages. Sometimes Ted's way proved the better, sometimes Mr. Turner's. Whichever plan promised to bring the more successful results was followed without regard for the years of him who had sponsored it. They were working together and for the same goal and what did it matter which of them had proposed the scheme they finally followed? To get the work completed and lay low the obstacles in their path were the only issues of importance.

So it was now. Things at Aldercliffe and Pine Lea must be done and done well, and only what furthered that end counted. Nevertheless, Ted would not have been a human boy had he not been pleased when some idea of his was adopted and found to be of use; this triumph, however, was less because the programme followed was his own than because it put forward the enterprise in hand. There was a satisfaction in finding the key to a balking problem and see it cease to be a problem. It was fun, for example, to think about the potatoes and then say to Mr. Wharton:

"Do you know, Mr. Wharton, I believe if we tried a different spray on that crop that isn't doing well it might help matters."

And when the new concoction was tried and it did help matters, what a glow of happiness came with the success!

What wonder that as the days passed, the niche awarded the lad grew bigger and bigger!

"There is no way you could come up here and live, is there, Ted?" Mr. Wharton inquired one day. "I'd give a good deal to have you here on the spot. Sometimes I want to talk with you outside working hours and I can't for the life of me lay hands on you. It's the deuce of a way to Freeman's Falls and you have no telephone. If you were here——" He paused meditatively, then continued, "There's a little shack down by the river which isn't in use. You may remember seeing it. It was started years ago as a boathouse for Mr. Laurie's canoes and then—well, it was never finished. It came to me the other day that we might clean it up, get some furnishings, and let you have it. How would the notion strike you?"

Ted's eyes sparkled.

"I'd like it of all things, sir!" returned he instantly.

"You wouldn't be timid about sleeping off there by yourself?"

"No, indeed!"

"Well, well! I had no idea you would listen to such a plan, much less like it. Suppose you go down there to-day and over-haul the place. Find out what would be required to make you comfortable and we will see what we can do about it. I should want you fixed up so you would be all right, you know. While we could not afford to go into luxuries, there would be no need for you to put up with makeshifts."

"But I am quite used to roughing it," protested Ted. "I've often camped out."

"Camping is all very well for a while but after a time it ceases to be a joke. No, if you move up here to accommodate us, you must have decent quarters. Both Mr. Fernald and Mr. Clarence would insist on that, I am certain. So make sure that the cabin is tight and write down what you think it would be necessary for you to have. Then we'll see about getting the things for you."

"You are mighty good, sir."

"Nonsense! It is for our own convenience," Mr. Wharton replied gruffly.

"Shall I—do you mean that I am to go over there after work to-night?"

"No. Go now. Cut along right away."

"But I was to help Mr. Stevens with the——"

"Stevens will have to get on without you. Tell him so from me. You can say I've set you at another job."

With springing step Ted hurried away. He was not sorry to exchange the tedious task of hoeing corn for the delightful one of furnishing a domicile for himself. What sport it would be to have at last a place which he could call his own! He could bring his books from home, his box of electrical things—all his treasures—and settle down in his kingdom like a young lord. He did not care at all if he had only a hammock to sleep in. The great satisfaction would be to be his own master and monarch of his own realm, no matter how tiny it was. Like lightning his imagination sped from one dream to another. If only Mr. Wharton would let him run some wires from the barn to the shack, what electrical contrivances he could rig up! He could then light the room and heat it, too; he could even cook by electricity.

Probably, however, Mr. Wharton would consider such a notion out of the question and much too ambitious. Even

SOON HE CAME WITHIN SIGHT OF THE SHACK WHICH STOOD AT THE WATER'S EDGE.

though the Fernalds had an electrical plant of their own, such a luxury was not to be thought of. A candle would do for lighting, of course.

Busy with these thoughts and others like them he sped across the meadow and through the woods toward the river. He was not content to walk the distance but like a child leaped and ran with an impatience not to be curbed. Soon he came within sight of the shack which stood at the water's edge, mid-way between Aldercliffe and Pine Lea, and was sheltered from view by a grove of thick pines. Its bare, boarded walls had silvered from exposure to the weather until it was scarcely noticeable against the gray tree trunks. Nevertheless, its crude, rough sides, its staring windows, and its tarred roof looked cheerless and deserted enough. But for Ted Turner it possessed none of these forbidding qualities. Instead of being a hermitage it seemed a paradise, a fairy kingdom, the castle of a knight's tale!

Thrusting the key which Mr. Wharton had given him into the padlock, he rolled open the sliding door and intermingled odors of cedar, tar, and paint greeted him. The room was of good size and was neatly sheathed as an evident preparation for receiving a finish of stain which, however, had never been put on. There were four large windows closed in by lights of glass, a rough board floor, and a fireplace of field stone. Everywhere was dirt, cobwebs, sawdust, and shavings; and scattered about so closely there was scarcely space to step was a litter of nails, fragments of boards, and a conglomeration of tin cans of various sizes.

Almost any one who beheld the chaos would have turned away discouraged. But not so Ted! The disorder was of no consequence in his eyes. Through all its dinginess and confusion he saw that the roof was tight, the windows whole, and the interior quite capable of being swept out, scrubbed and put in order. That was all he wanted to know. Why, the place could be made into a little heaven! Already he could see it transformed into a dwelling of the utmost comfort. He had remodelled many a worse spot,—the barn loft in Vermont, for example, and made it habitable. One had only to secure a table, a chair or two, build a bunk and get a mattress, and the trick was turned.

How proud he should be to have such a dwelling for his own!

He could hardly restrain himself from rolling up his sleeves and going to work then and there. Fearing, however, that Mr. Wharton might be awaiting his report, he reluctantly closed the door again, turned the key in it, and hurried back to the manager's office.

"Well," inquired the elder man, spinning around in his desk chair as the boy entered and noting the glow in the youthful face, "how did you find things at the shack? Any hope in the place?"

"Hope!" repeated Ted. "Why, sir, the house is corking! Of course, it is dirty now but I could clean it up and put it in bully shape. All I'd need would be to build a bunk, get a few pieces of furniture, and the place would be cosy as anything. If you'll say the word, I'll start right in to-night after work and——"

"Why wait until to-night?" came drily from the manager.

"Why—er—I thought perhaps—you see there is the corn——"

"Never mind the corn," Mr. Wharton interrupted.

"You mean I could go right ahead now?" asked Ted eagerly.

"Certainly. You are doing this for our accommodation, not for your own, and there is no earthly reason why you should perform the work outside your regular hours."

"But it is for my accommodation, too," put in the lad with characteristic candor.

"I am very glad if it happens to be," nodded Mr. Wharton. "So much the better. But at any rate, you are not going to take your recreation time for the job. Now before you go, tell me your ideas as to furnishings. You will need some things, of course."

"Not much," Ted answered quickly. "As I said, I can knock together a bunk and rough table myself. If I could just have a couple of chairs——"

Mr. Wharton smiled at the modesty of the request.

"Suppose we leave the furnishing until later," said he, turning back to his desk with a gesture of dismissal. "I may drop round there some time to-day while you're working. We can then decide more fully upon what is necessary. You'll find brooms, mops, rags, and water in the barn, you know. Now be off. I'm busy."

Away went Ted, only too eager to obey. In no time he was laden with all the paraphernalia he desired. He stopped at Stevens' cottage only long enough to add to his equipment a pail of steaming water and then, staggering under the weight of his burden of implements, made his way to the shack. Once there he threw off his coat, removed his collar and tie, rolled up his sleeves, and went to work. First he cleared the bulk of rubbish from the room and set it outside; then he swept up the floor and mopped it with hot suds; afterwards he washed the windows and rubbed them until they shone. Often he had watched his mother and sisters, who were well trained New England housekeepers, perform similar offices and therefore he knew exactly how such things should be done. It took him a solid morning to render the interior spotless and just as he was pausing to view his handiwork with weary satisfaction Mr. Wharton came striding in at the door.

"Mercy on us!" gasped the newcomer with amazement.

"You have been busy! Why, I had no idea there were such possibilities in this place. The room is actually a pretty one, isn't it? We shall be able to fix you up snug as a bug in a rug here." He ran his eye quickly about. "If you put your bunk between the windows, you will get plenty of air. You'll need window shades, some comfortable chairs, a bureau, a table———"

"I think I can make a table myself," Ted put in timidly. "That is, if I can have some boards."

"No, no, no! There are boards enough. But you don't want a makeshift thing like that. If you are going to have books and perhaps read or study, you must have something that will stand solidly on four legs. I may be able to root a table out of some corner. Then there will be bedding———"

"I can bring that from home."

"All right. We'll count on you to supply that if you are sure you have it to spare. I'll be responsible for the rest." He stopped an instant to glance into the boy's face then added kindly, "So you think you are going to like your new quarters, eh?"

"You bet I am!"

"That's good! And by the by, I have arranged for you to have your meals with Stevens and his wife. They like you and were glad to take you in. Only you must be prompt and not make them wait for you. Should you prove yourself a bother they might turn you out."

"I'll be on hand, sir."

"See that you are. They have breakfast at seven, dinner at twelve, and supper at six. Whenever you decide to spend Sunday with your family, or take any meals elsewhere, you must, of course, be thoughtful enough to announce beforehand that you are to be away."

"Yes, sir."

Ted waited a few moments and then, as Mr. Wharton appeared to be on the point of leaving, he asked with hesitancy:

"How—how—much will my meals cost?"

An intonation of anxiety rang in the question.

"Your meals are our hunt," Mr. Wharton replied instantly. "We shall see to those."

"But—but——"

"You'll be worth your board to the Fernald estates, never fear, my lad; so put it all out of your mind and don't think of it any more. All is, should we ask of you some little extra service now and then, I am sure you will willingly perform it, won't you?"

"Sure!" came with emphatic heartiness.

"Then I don't see but everything is settled," the manager declared, as he started back through the grove of pines. "I gave orders up at the toolhouse that you were to have whatever boards, nails, and tools you wanted, so don't hesitate to sail in and hunt up anything you need."

"You are mighty kind, sir."

"Pooh, pooh. Nonsense! Aren't you improving the Fernald property, I'd like to know?" Mr. Wharton laughed. "This boat-house has been an eyesore for years. We shall be glad enough to have it fixed up and used for something."

CHAPTER IV

THE FIRST NIGHT IN THE SHACK

Throughout the long summer afternoon Ted worked on, fitting up his new quarters. Not only did he make a comfortable bunk for himself such as he had frequently constructed when at logging or sugaring-off camps in Vermont, but having several boards left he built along the racks originally intended for canoes some shelves for the books he meant to bring from home. By late afternoon he had finished all it was possible for him to do and he decided to go to Freeman's Falls and join his own family at supper, and while there collect the possessions he wished to transfer to the shack.

Accordingly he washed up and started out.

It was a little late when he reached the house and already his father and sisters were at table.

"Mercy on us, Ted, what under the sun have you been doing until this time of night?" demanded Mr. Turner. "I should call from seven in the morning until seven at night a pretty long day."

"Oh, I haven't been working all this time," laughed the boy. "Or at least, if I have, I have been having the time of my life doing it."

Eagerly, and with youthful enthusiasm, he poured out the tale of the day's happenings while the others listened.

"So you are starting out housekeeping, are you?" chuckled Mr.

Turner, when the narrative was finished. "It certainly ain't a bad idea. Not that we're glad to get rid of you—although I will admit we ain't got the room here that I wish we had. It is the amount of time you'll save and the strength, too, that I'm thinking of. It must be a good three miles up to Aldercliffe and Pine Lea is at least two miles farther. Being on the spot is going to make a lot of difference. But how are you going to get along? What will you do for food? I ain't going to have you eating stuff out of tin cans."

"Oh, you needn't worry about me, Dad. Mr. Wharton has arranged for me to take my meals with Mr. and Mrs. Stevens who have a cottage on the place. Stevens is the head farmer, you know."

"A pretty penny that will cost you! What does the man think you are—a millionaire?"

"Mr. Wharton told me the Fernalds would see to the bill."

"Oh! That's another matter," ejaculated Mr. Turner, entirely mollified. "I will say it's pretty decent of Mr. Wharton. Seems to me he is doing a good deal for you."

"Yes, he is."

"Well, all is you must do your full share in return so he won't lose anything by it." The elder man paused thoughtfully. "Ain't there anything we could do to help out? Perhaps we could donate something toward your furnishings."

"Mr. Wharton said if I could supply my own bedding——"

"We certainly can do that," put in Ruth quickly. "There is a trunkful of extra comforters and blankets in the back room that I should be thankful enough to ship off somewhere else. And wouldn't you like some curtains? Seems to me they'd make it cosy and homelike. I've a piece of old chintz we've never used. Why not make it into curtains and do away with buying window shades?"

"That would be great!"

"It would be lots more cheerful," remarked Nancy. "What kind of a bed have you got?"

"I've built a wooden bunk-two bunks, in fact—one over the other like the berths in a ship. I thought perhaps sometime Dad might want to come up and visit me; and while I was at it, it was no more work to make two beds than one."

Mr. Turner smiled in friendly fashion into his son's eyes. The two were great pals and it pleased him that the lad should have included him in his plans.

"Beds like that will do all very well for a night or two; but for a steady thing they will be darned uncomfortable. Cover 'em with pine boughs after a long tramp through the woods and they seem like heaven; but try 'em day after day and they cease to be a joke. Wasn't there a wire spring round here somewhere, Ruth? Seems to me I remember it standing up against something. Why wouldn't that be the very thing? You could fasten it in place and have a bed good as you have at home."

"That's a corking idea, Dad!"

"I wish we could go up and see the place," Ruth suggested. "I am crazy to know what it looks like. Besides, I want to measure the windows."

"Maybe we could run up there to-night," her father replied rising. "It is not late and the Maguires said they would take us out for a little spin in their Ford before dark. They might enjoy riding up to Aldercliffe and be quite willing we should take along the spring bed. Mat is a kind soul and I haven't a doubt he'd be glad to do us a favor. Run down and ask him, Ted; or wait—I'll go myself."

The Maguires had the apartment just below the Turner's and Mat, a thrifty and good-humored Irishman, was one of the night watchmen at the Fernald mills. He had a plump little wife, but as there were no children he had been able to save more money than had some of his neighbors, and in consequence had purchased a small car which it was his delight to use for the benefit of his friends. In fact, he often called it the Maguire jitney, and the joke never became threadbare to his simple mind, for every time he made it he laughed as heartily as if he had never heard it before, and so did everybody else. Therefore no sooner had Mr. Turner proposed his plan than Mat was all eagerness to further the project.

"Sure I'll take you—as many of you as can pile in, and the spring bed, too! If you don't mind the inconvenience of the luggage, I don't. And tell Ted to bring along anything else he'd like to carry. We can pack you all in and the stuff on top of you. 'Twill be easy enough. Just make ready as soon as you can, so the dark won't catch us."

You may be sure the Turners needed no second bidding. Ruth and Nancy scrambled the supper dishes out of the way while Ted and his father hauled the wire spring out, brushed it, and dragged it downstairs. Afterward Ted collected his box of electrical treasures, his books, and clothing. What he would do with all these things he did not stop to inquire. The chance to transfer them was at hand and he seized it with avidity. His belongings might as well be stored in the shack as anywhere else,—better, far better, for the space they left behind would be very welcome to the Turner household.

Therefore with many a laugh, the party crowded into the waiting car and set out for Aldercliffe; and when at length they arrived at the house in the pines and Ted unlocked the sliding doors and pushed them wide open, ushering in his guests, what a landholder he felt!

"My, but this is a tidy little place!" Maguire ejaculated. "And it's not so little, either. Why, it's a regular palace! Look at the fireplace and the four windows! My eye! And the tier of bunks is neat as a ship's cabin. Bear a hand here with the spring. I'm all of a quaver to see if it fits," cried the man.

"I made the bunks regulation size, so I guess there won't be any trouble about that," Ted answered.

"The head on the lad!" the Irishman cried. "Ain't he the brainy one, though? You don't catch him wool-gathering! Not he!"

Nevertheless he was not content until the spring had been hoisted into place and he saw with his own eyes that it was exactly the proper size. "Could anything be cuter!" observed he with satisfaction. "Now with a good mattress atop of that you will have a bed fit for a king. You'll be comfortable as if you were in a solid gold bedstead, laddie!"

"I'm afraid I may be too comfortable," laughed Ted. "What if I should oversleep and not get to breakfast, or to work, on time!"

"That would never do," Mr. Turner said promptly. "You must have an alarm clock. 'Twould be but a poor return for Mr. Wharton's kindness were you to come dawdling to work."

"I guess you can trust Ted to be on time," put in Ruth soothingly. "He is seldom late—especially to *meals*. Even if he were to be late at other places, I should always be sure he would show up when there was anything to eat."

"You bet I would," announced the boy, with a good-humored grin.

"I shall have enough chintz for curtains for all your windows," interrupted Nancy, who had been busy taking careful measurements during the conversation. "We'll get some brass rods and make the hangings so they will slip back and forth easily; they will be much nicer than window shades."

"Ain't there nothin' I can donate?" inquired Mat Maguire anxiously. "A rag rug, now—why wouldn't that be a good thing? The missus makes 'em by the dozen and our house is full of 'em. We're breakin' our necks mornin', noon, and night on 'em. A couple to lay down here wouldn't be so bad, I'm thinking. You could put one beside your bed and another before the door to wipe your feet on. They'd cheer the room up as well as help keep you warm. Just say the word, sonny, and you shall have 'em."

"I'd like them tremendously."

The kind-hearted Irishman beamed with pleasure.

"Sure, they'll be better out of our house than in it," remarked he, trying to conceal his gratification. "You can try stumbling over 'em a spell instead of me. 'Twill be interesting to see which of us breaks his neck first."

It was amazing to see how furniture came pouring in at Ted's bachelor quarters during the next few days. The chintz curtains were finished and hung; the Maguire rugs made their appearance; Mr. Turner produced a shiny alarm clock; and Nancy a roll of colored prints which she had cut from the magazines.

"You'll be wanting some pictures," said she. "Tack these up somewhere. They'll brighten up the room and cover the bare walls."

Thus it was that day by day the wee shack in the woods became more cheery and homelike.

"I've managed to hunt up a few trap's for you," called Mr. Wharton one morning, as he met the boy going to work. "If you want to run over to the cabin now and unlock the door, I'll send a man over with them."

Want to! Ted was off in a second, impatient to see what new treasures he was to receive. He had not long to wait, for soon one of the farm trucks came into sight, and the driver began to deposit its contents on the wooden platform which sloped from the door down to the river.

As Ted helped the man unload, his eyes shone with delight. Could any gifts be rarer? To be sure the furniture was not new. In fact, some of it was old and even shabby with wear. But the things were all whole, and although they were simple they were serviceable and perhaps looked more in harmony with the old-fashioned curtains and the quaint rugs than if they had come fresh from the shop. There was a chest of drawers; a rocking chair, a leather armchair, and a straight wooden chair; a mirror with frame of faded gilt; a good-sized wooden table; and, best of all, a much scarred, flat-topped desk. Ted had never owned a desk in all his life. Often he had dreamed of sitting behind one when he grew to be a man. But to have it now—here! To have it for his own! How it thrilled him!

After the furniture was in place and the teamster had gone, he arranged his few papers and pencils in the desk draw-ers a score of times, trying them first in one spot and then in another. It was marvelous how much room there was in such an article of furniture. What did men use to fill up such a mighty receptacle, anyway? Stretch his possessions as he would, they only made a scattered showing at the bottom of three of the drawers. He laughed to see them lying there and hear them rattle about when he brought the drawers to with a click. However, it was very splendid to have a desk, whether one had anything to put in it or not, and perhaps in time he would be able to collect more pencils, rulers and blocks of paper. The contrast between not having any room at all for his things and then so much that he did not know what to do with it was amusing.

Now at last he was fully equipped to take up residence in his new abode and every instant he could snatch from his duties that day he employed in settling his furniture, making up his bed, filling his water pitcher from the river and completing his final preparations for residence at the boathouse. That night he moved in.

Nothing had been omitted that would contribute to his comfort. Mr. Wharton had given him screens for the windows and across the broad door he had tacked a curtain of netting that could be dropped or pushed aside at will. The candlelight glowing from a pair of old brass candlesticks on the shelf above the fireplace contributed rather than took away from the effect and to his surprise the room assumed under the mellow radiance a quality actually æsthetic and beautiful.

"I don't believe Aldercliffe or Pine Lea have anything better than this to offer," the boy murmured aloud, as he looked about him with pride. "I'd give anything to have Mr. Wharton see it now that it's done!"

Strangely enough, the opportunity to exhibit his kingdom followed on the very heels of his desire, for while he was arranging the last few books he had brought from home on the shelf above his desk he heard a tap at the door.

"Are you in bed, son?" called the manager. "I saw your light and just dropped round to see if you had everything you wanted."

Rushing to the door, Ted threw it open.

"I haven't begun to go to bed yet," returned he. "I've been too excited. How kind of you to come!"

"Curiosity! Curiosity!" responded the man hastily. Although Ted knew well that the comment was a libel, he laughed as Mr. Wharton came in, drawing the door together behind him.

"By Jove!" burst out the manager, glancing about the room. "You like it?"

"Why—what in goodness have you done to the place? I—I—mercy on us!"

"You do like it then?" the boy insisted eagerly.

"Like it! Why, you've made it into a regular little palace. I'd no idea such a thing was possible. Where did you get your candlesticks and your andirons?"

"From home. We have radiators in the apartment and so my sisters had stored them away and were only too glad to have me take them."

"Humph! And your curtains came from home, too?"

"Yes, sir."

"Well, you've missed your calling, is all I can say. You belong in the interior decorating business," asserted Mr. Wharton. "Wait until Mr. Clarence sees this place." Again the elder man looked critically round the interior. "I wouldn't mind living here myself—hanged if I would. The only thing I don't like is those candles. There is a good deal of a draught here and you are too near the pines to risk a fire. Electricity would be safer."

Whistling softly to himself, he began to walk thoughtfully about.

"I suppose," he presently went on, "it would be a simple enough matter to run wires over here from the barn."

"Wouldn't that be bully!"

"You'd like it?"

"Yes, siree!"

The manager took up his hat.

"Well, we'll see what can be done," he answered, moving toward the door.

But on the threshold he stopped once more and looked about.

"I'm going to bring some of the Fernalds over here to see

the place," observed he. "For some time Mr. Clarence has been complaining that this shack was a blot on the estate and threatening to pull it down. He'd better have a peep at it now. You may find he'll be taking it away from you."

He saw a startled look leap into the boy's eyes.

"No, no, sonny! Have no fears. I was only joking," he added. "Nevertheless, the house will certainly be a surprise to anybody who saw it a week ago. I wouldn't have believed such a transformation was possible."

Then as he disappeared with his flash-light through the windings of the pine woods he called:

"We'll see about that electric wiring. I imagine it won't be much of a job, and I should breathe easier to eliminate those candles, pretty as they are. Until something is done, just be careful not to set yourself and us afire!"

With that he was gone.

Ted dropped the screen and loitered a moment in the doorway, looking out into the night. Before him stretched the river; so near was it that he could hear the musical lappings of its waters among the tall grasses that bordered the stream. From the ground, matted thickly with pine needles, rose a warm, sun-scorched fragrance heavy with sleep.

The boy stretched his arms and yawned. Then he rolled the doors together and began to undress.

Suddenly he paused with one shoe in his hand. A thought had come to him. If Mr. Wharton ran the electric wires over to the shack, what was to prevent him from utilizing the current for some of his own contrivances? Why, he could, perhaps, put his wireless instruments into operation and rig up a telephone in his little dwelling. What fun it would be to unearth his treasures from the big wooden box in which they had been so long packed away and set them up here where they would interfere with no one but himself!

He hoped with all his heart the manager would continue to be nervous about those candles.

CHAPTER V

A VISITOR

Fervent as this wish was, it was several days before Ted saw Mr. Wharton again and in the meantime the boy began to adapt himself to his new mode of living with a will. His alarm clock got him up in the morning in time for a plunge in the river and after a brisk rub-down he was off to breakfast with the Stevens's, whose cottage was one of a tiny colony of bungalows where lived the chauffeurs, head gardener, electricians, and others who held important positions on the two estates.

It did not take many days for Ted to become thoroughly at home in the pretty cement house where he discovered many slight services he could perform for Mrs. Stevens during the scraps of leisure left him after meals. His farm training had rendered him very handy with tools and he was quick to see little things which needed to be done. Moreover, the willingness to help, which from the moment of his advent to Aldercliffe and Pine Lea had made him a favorite with Mr. Wharton and the men, speedily won for him a place with the kindly farmer's wife.

Had Ted known it, she had been none too well pleased at the prospect of adopting into her home a ravenous young lad who might, nay, probably would be untidy and troublesome; but she did not dare oppose Mr. Wharton when the plan was suggested.

Nevertheless, although she consented, she grumbled not a little to her husband about the inconvenience of the scheme. The money offered her by the manager had been the only redeeming factor in the case. Quite ignorant of these conditions, Ted had made his advent into the house and she soon found to her amazement that the daily coming of her cheery boarder became an event which she anticipated with motherly interest.

"He is such a well-spoken boy and so nice to have round," asserted she to Mr. Wharton. "Not a mite of trouble, either. In fact, he's a hundred times handier than my own man, who although he can make a garden thrive can't drive a nail straight to save his life. And there's never any fussing about his food. He eats everything and enjoys it. I believe Stevens and I were getting dreadful pokey all alone here by ourselves. The lad has brightened us up no end. We wouldn't part with him now for anything."

Thus it was that Ted Turner made his way. His password was usefulness. He never measured the hours he worked by the clock, never was too busy or too tired to fill in a gap; and although he was popular with everybody, and a favorite with those in authority, he never took advantage of his position to escape toil or obtain privileges. In fact, he worked harder if anything than did the other men, and as soon as his associates saw that the indulgence granted him did not transform him into a pig, they ceased any jealousy they cherished and accorded him their cordial goodwill. For Ted was always modestly respectful toward older persons; and if he knew more about farming and some other things than did a good many of the laborers on the place, he did not push himself forward or boast of his superiority.

Consequently when he ventured to say, "I wonder if somebody would help me with this harrow?" he would receive a dozen eager responses, the men never suspecting that Mr. Wharton had given this little chap authority to order them to aid with the harrowing of the field. Instead each workman thought his cooperation a free-will offering and enjoyed giving it.

Thus a fortnight passed and no one could have been happier than was Ted Turner on a certain clear June evening. He had finished his Saturday night supper of baked beans and brown bread and after it was over had lingered to feed the Stevens's hens, in order to let Mr. Stevens go early to Freeman's Falls to purchase the Sunday dinner. As a result, it was later than usual when he started out for his camp on the river's brink. The long, busy day was over; he was tired and the prospect of his comfortable bed was very alluring. It was some distance to the shack, and before he was halfway through the pine woods that separated Aldercliffe from Pine Lea darkness had fallen, and he was compelled to move cautiously along the narrow, curving trail. How black the night was! A storm must be brewing, thought he, as he glanced up into the starless heavens. Stumbling over the rough and slippery ground on he went. Then suddenly he rounded a turn in the path and stood arrested with terror.

Not more than a rod away, half concealed in the denseness of the sweeping branches rose his little shack, a blaze of light! A wave of consternation turned him cold and two solutions of the mystery immediately flashed into his mind—fire and marauders. Either something had ignited in the interior of the house; or, since it was isolated and had long been known to be vacant, strolling mischief-makers had broken in and were ransacking it. He remembered now that he had left a window open when he had gone off in the morning. Doubtless thieves were at this moment busy appropriating his possessions. Of course it could not be any of the Fernald workmen. They were too friendly and honorable to commit such a dastardly deed. No, it was some one from outside. Was it not possible men had come down the river in a boat from Melton, the village above, and spying the house had made a landing and encamped there for the night?

Well, live or die, he must know who his unwelcome guests were. It would be cowardly to leave them in possession of the place and make no attempt to discover their identity. For that invaders were inside the shack he was now certain. It was not a fire. There was neither smoke nor flame. Softly he crept nearer, the thick matting of pine needles muffling his footsteps. But how his heart beat! Suppose a twig should crack beneath his feet and warn the vandals of his approach? And suppose they rushed out, caught him, and—for a moment he halted with fear; then, summoning every particle of courage he possessed, he tiptoed on and contrived to reach one of the windows.

There he halted, staring, his knees weak from surging reaction.

Instead of the company of bandits his mind had pictured, there in the rocker sat Mr. Wharton and opposite him, in the great leather armchair, was Mr. Clarence Fernald. The latter fact would have been astounding enough. But the marvel did not cease there. The light suffusing the small room came from no flickering candles but glowed steadily from two strong, unblinking electric lights, one of which had been connected with a low lamp on his desk, and the other with a fixture in the ceiling.

Ted could scarcely believe his eyes. All day, during his absence, electricians must have been busy. How carefully they had guarded their secret. Why, he had talked with Tim Toyer that very morning on his way to work and Tim had breathed no word, although he was the head electrician and had charge of the dynamo which generated the current both for Aldercliffe and Pine Lea. The Fernalds had never depended on Freeman's Falls for their electricity; on the contrary, they maintained a small plant of their own and used the power for a score of purposes on the two estates.

Evidently either Mr. Wharton or Mr. Clarence Fernald himself must have given the order which had with such Aladdin-like magic been so promptly and mysteriously fulfilled. It certainly was kind of them to do this and Ted determined they should not find him wanting in gratitude. Pocketing his shyness, he opened the door and stepped into the room. "Well, youngster, I thought it was about time the host made his appearance," exclaimed Mr. Wharton. "We could not have waited much longer. Mr. Fernald, this is Ted Turner, the lad I have been telling you about."

Ted waited.

The mill-owner nodded, let his eye travel over the boy's flushed face, and then, as if satisfied by what he saw there, he put out his hand.

"I have been hearing very excellent reports of you, Turner," said he, "and I wished to investigate for myself the quarters they have given you to live in. You've made a mighty shipshape little den of this place."

"It didn't need very much done to it," protested Ted, blushing under the fixed gaze of the great man. "I just cleaned it up and arranged the furniture. Mr. Wharton was kind enough to give me most of it."

"I can't claim any thanks," laughed the manager. "The traps I gave you were all cast-offs and not in use. It is what you have done with them that is the marvel."

"You certainly have turned your donations to good purpose," Mr. Fernald observed. "I've been noticing your books in your absence and see that most of them are textbooks on electricity. I judge you are interested in that sort of thing."

"Yes, sir, I am."

"Humph!"

The financier drummed reflectively on the arm of his chair.

"How did you happen to go into that?" he asked presently.

"I have been studying it at school. My father is letting me go through the high school—at least he hopes to let me finish my course there. I have been two years already. That is why I am working during the summer."

"I see. And so you have been taking up electricity at school, eh?"

"Yes, sir. I really am taking a business course. The science work in the laboratory is an extra that I just run in because I like it. My father wanted me to fit myself for business. He thought it would be better for me," explained Ted.

"But you prefer the science?"

"I am afraid I do, sir," smiled Ted, with ingratiating honesty. "But I don't mean to let it interfere with my regular work. I try to remember it is only a side issue."

Mr. Clarence Fernald did not answer and during his interval of silence Ted fell to speculating on what he was thinking. Probably the magnate was disapproving of his still going to school and was saying to himself how much better it would have been had he been put into the mill and trained up there instead of having his head stuffed with stenography and electrical knowledge.

"What did you do in electricity?" the elder man asked at length.

"Oh, I fussed around some with telephones, wireless, and telegraph instruments."

Mr. Fernald smiled.

"Did you get where you could take messages?" inquired he with real interest.

"By telegraph?"

The financier nodded.

"I did a little at it," replied Ted. "Of course I was slow."

"And what about wireless?"

"I got on better with that. I rigged up a small receiving station at home but when the war came I had to take it down."

"So that outfit was yours, was it?" commented Mr. Fernald. "I noticed it one day when I was in the village. What luck did you have with it?"

"Oh, I contrived to pick up messages within a short radius. My outfit wasn't very powerful."

"I suppose not. And the telephone?"

They saw an eager light leap into the lad's eyes.

"I've worked more at that than anything else," replied he. "You see one of the instruments at the school gave out and they set me to tinkering at it. In that way I got tremendously interested in it. Afterward some of us fellows did some experimenting and managed to concoct a crude one in the laboratory. It wasn't much of a telephone but we finally got it to work."

"They tell me you are a good farmer as well as an electrician," Mr. Fernald said.

"Oh, I was brought up on a farm, sir."

The great man rose.

"Well, mind you don't let your electricity make you forget your farming," cautioned he, not unkindly. "We need you right where you are. Still I will own electricity is a pleasant pastime. You will have a current to work with now whenever you want to play with it. Just be sure you don't get a short circuit and blow out my dynamo."

"Do—do—you really mean I may use the current for experiments?" demanded Ted.

Whether Mr. Fernald had made his remarks in jest or expected them to be taken seriously was not apparent; and if he were surprised at having the boy catch him up and hold him to account, he at least displayed not a trace of being taken unawares. For only an instant was he thoughtful, and that was while he paused and studied the countenance of the lad before him.

"Why, I don't know that I see any harm in your using the current for reasonable purposes," he answered slowly, after an interval of meditation. "You understand the dangers of running too many volts through your body and of crossing wires, don't you?"

"Oh, yes, sir," laughed Ted.

"I must confess I should not trust every boy with such a plaything," continued the magnate, "but you seem to have a good head on your shoulders and I guess we can take a chance on you." He moved silently across the room but on the threshold he turned and added with self-conscious hesitancy, "By the way my—my—son, Mr. Laurie, chances to be interested in electricity, too. Perhaps some day he might drop in here and have a talk about this sort of thing."

"I wish he would."

With a quiet glance the father seemed to thank the lad for his simple and natural reply. Both of them knew but too well that such an event could never be a casual happening, and that if poor Mr. Laurie ever *dropped in* at the shack it would be only when he was brought there, either in his wheel-chair or in the arms of some of the servants from Pine Lea. Nevertheless it was obvious that Mr. Fernald appreciated the manner in which Ted ignored these facts and suppressed his surprise at the unusual suggestion. Had Mr. Laurie's dropping in been an ordinary occurrence no one could have treated it with less ceremony than did Ted.

An echo of the gratitude the capitalist felt lingered in his voice when he said good night. It was both gentle and husky with emotion and the lad fell asleep marvelling that the men employed at the mills should assert that the Fernalds were frigid and snobby.

CHAPTER VI

MORE GUESTS

When with shining eyes Ted told his father about Mr. Fernald's visit to the shack, Mr. Turner simply shrugged his shoulders and smiled indulgently.

"Likely Mr. Clarence's curiosity got the better of him," said he, "and he wanted to look your place over and see that it warn't too good; or mebbe he just happened to be going by. He never would have taken the trouble to go that far out of his way if he hadn't had something up his sleeve. When men like him are too pleasant, I'm afraid of 'em. And as for Mr. Laurie *dropping in*—why, his father and grandfather would no more let him associate with folks like us than they'd let him jump headfirst into the river. We ain't good enough for the Fernalds. Probably almost nobody on earth is. And when it comes to Mr. Laurie, why, in their opinion the boy doesn't live who is fit to sit in the same room with him."

Ted's bright face clouded with disappointment.

"I never thought of Mr. Laurie feeling like that," answered he.

"Oh, I ain't saying Mr. Laurie himself is so high and mighty. He ain't. The poor chap has nothing to be high and mighty about and he knows it. Anybody who is as dependent on others as he is can't afford to tilt his nose up in the air and put on lugs. For all I know to the contrary he may be simple as a baby. It's his folks that think he's the king-pin and keep him in cotton wool." Mr. Turner paused, his lip curling with scorn. "You'll never see Mr. Laurie at your shack, mark my words. His people would not let him come even if he wanted to."

The light of eagerness in his son's countenance died entirely.

"I suppose you're right," admitted he slowly and with evident reluctance.

Although he would not have confessed it, he had been anticipating, far more than he would have been willing to own, the coming of Mr. Laurie. Over and over again he had lived in imagination his meeting with this fairy prince whose grave, wistful face and pleasant smile had so strongly attracted him. He had speculated to himself as to what the other boy was like and had coveted the chance to speak to him, never realizing that they were not on an equal plane. Mr. Fernald's suggestion of Laurie visiting the shack seemed the most natural thing in the world, and immediately after it had been made Ted's fancy had run riot, and he had leaped beyond the first formal preliminaries to a time when he and Laurie Fernald would really know one another, even come to be genuine friends, perhaps. What sport two lads, interested in the same things, could have together!

Ted had few companions who followed the bent of thought that he did. The fellows he knew either at school or in the town were ready enough to play football and baseball but almost none of them, for example, wanted to sacrifice a pleasant Saturday to constructing a wireless outfit. One or two of them, it is true, had begun the job but they soon tired of it and either sat down to watch him work or had deserted him altogether. The only congenial companion he had been able to count on had been the young assistant in the laboratory at school who, although he was not at all aged, was nevertheless years older than Ted.

But with the mention of Mr. Laurie myriad dreams had flashed into his mind. Here was no prim old scholar but a lad like himself, who probably did not know much more about electrical matters than he. You wouldn't feel ashamed to admit your ignorance before such a person, or own that you either did not know, or did not understand. You could blunder along with such a companion to your heart's content. Such had been his belief until now, with a dozen words, Ted saw his father shatter the illusion. No, of course Mr. Laurie would never come to the shack. It had been absurd to think it for a moment. And even if he did, it would only be as a lofty and unapproachable spectator. Mr. Fernald's words were a subtly designed flattery intended to put him in good humor because he wanted something of him.

What could it be?

Perhaps he meant to oust him out of the boathouse and rebuild it, or possibly tear it down; or maybe he had taken a fancy to use it as it was and desired to be rid of Ted in some sort of pleasant fashion. Unquestionably the building belonged to Mr. Fernald and if he chose to reclaim it he had a perfect right to do so.

Poor Ted! With a crash his air castles tumbled about his ears and the ecstasy of his mood gave way to apprehension and unhappiness. Each day he waited, expecting to hear through Mr. Wharton that Mr. Clarence Fernald had decided to use the shack for other purposes. Time slipped along, however, and no such tidings came. In the meanwhile Mr. Wharton made no further mention of the Fernalds and gradually Ted's fears calmed down sufficiently for him to gain confidence enough to unpack his boxes of wire, his tools, and instruments. Nevertheless, in spite of this, his first enthusiasm had seeped away and he did not attempt to go farther than to take the things out and look at them.

Before his father had withered his ambitions by his pessimism, a score of ideas had danced through his brain. He had thought of running a buzzer over to the Stevens's bungalow in order that Mrs. Stevens might ring for him when she wanted him; and he had thought of connecting Mr. Wharton's office with the shack by telephone. He felt sure he could do both these things and would have liked nothing better than try them. But now what was the use? If a little later on Mr. Fernald intended to take the shack away from him, it would be foolish to waste toil and material for nothing. For the present, at least, he much better hold off and see what happened.

Yet notwithstanding this resolve, he did continue to improve the appearance of the boathouse. Just why, he could not have told. Perhaps it was a vent for his disquietude. At any rate, having some scraps of board left and hearing the gardener say there were more geraniums in the greenhouse than he knew what to do with, Ted made some windowboxes for the Stevens's and himself, painted them green, and filled them with flowering plants. They really were very pretty and added a surprising touch of beauty to the dull, weather-stained little dwelling in the woods. Mr. Wharton was delighted and said so frankly.

"Your camp looks as attractive as a teahouse," said he. "You have no idea how gay the red flowers look among these dark pine trees. How came you to think of window-boxes?"

"Oh, I don't know," was Ted's reply. "The bits of board suggested it, I guess. Then Collins said the greenhouses were overstocked, and he seemed only too glad to get rid of his plants."

"I'll bet he was," responded Mr. Wharton. "If there is anything he hates, it is to raise plants and not have them used. He always has to start more slips than he needs in case some of them do not root; when they do, he is swamped. Evidently you have helped him solve his problem for no sooner did the owners of the other bungalows see Stevens's boxes than everybody wanted them. They all are pestering the carpenter for boards. It made old Mr. Fernald chuckle, for he likes flowers and is delighted to have the cottages on the place made attractive. He asked who started the notion; and when I told him it was you he said he had heard about you and wanted to see you some time."

This time Ted was less thrilled by the remark than he would have been a few days before. A faint degree of his father's scepticism had crept into him and the only reply he vouchsafed was a polite smile. It was absurd to fancy for an instant that the senior member of the Fernald company, the head of the firm, the owner of Aldercliffe, the great and rich Mr. Lawrence Fernald, would ever trouble himself to hunt up a boy who worked on the place. Ridiculous!

Yet it was on the very day that he made these positive and scornful assertions to himself that he found this same mighty Mr. Lawrence Fernald on his doorstep.

It was early Saturday afternoon, a time Ted always had for a holiday. He had not been to see his family for some time and he had made up his mind to start out directly after luncheon and go to Freeman's Falls, where he would, perhaps, remain overnight. Therefore he came swinging through the trees, latchkey in hand, and hurriedly rounding the corner of the shack, he almost jostled into the river Mr. Lawrence Fernald who was loitering on the platform before the door.

"I beg your pardon, sir!" he gasped. "I did not know any one was here."

"Nor did I, young man," replied the ruffled millionaire. "You came like a thief in the night."

"It is the pine needles, sir," explained the boy simply. "Unless you happen to step on a twig that cracks you don't hear a sound."

The directness of the lad evidently pleased the elder man for he answered more kindly:

"It is quiet here, isn't it? I did not know there was a spot within a radius of five miles that was so still. I was almost imagining myself in the heart of the Maine woods before you came."

"I never was in the Maine woods," ventured Ted timidly, "but if it is finer than this I'd like to see it."

"You like your quarters then?"

"Indeed I do, sir."

"And you're not afraid to stay way off here by yourself?"

"Oh, no!"

Mr. Fernald peered over the top of his glasses at the boy before him.

"Would you—would you care to come inside the shack?" Ted inquired after an interval of silence, during which Mr. Fernald had not taken his eyes from his face. "It is very cosy indoors—at least I think so."

"Since I am here I suppose I might just glance into the house," was the capitalist's rather magnificent retort. "I don't often get around to this part of the estate. To-day I followed the river and came farther away from Aldercliffe than I intended. When I got to this point the sun was so pleasant here on the float that I lingered."

Nodding, Ted fitted the key into the padlock, turned it, and rolled the doors apart, allowing Mr. Fernald to pass within. The mill owner was a large man and as he stalked about, peering at the fireplace with its andirons of wrought metal, examining the chintz hangings, and casting his eye over the books on the shelf, he seemed to fill the entire room. Then suddenly, having completed his circuit of the interior, he failed to bow himself out as Ted expected and instead dropped into the big leather armchair and proceeded to draw out a cigar.

"I suppose you don't mind if I smoke," said he, at the same instant lighting a match.

"Oh, no. Dad always smokes," replied the boy.

"Your father is in our shipping room, they tell me."

"Yes, sir."

"Where did you live before you came here?"

"Vermont."

"Vermont, eh?" commented the older man with interest. "I was born in Vermont."

"Were you?" Ted ejaculated. "I didn't know that."

"Yes, I was born in Vermont," mused Mr. Fernald slowly. "Born on a farm, as you no doubt were, and helped with the haying, milking, and other chores."

"There were plenty of them," put in the boy, forgetting for the moment whom he was addressing.

"That's right!" was the instant and hearty response. "There was precious little time left afterward for playing marbles or flying kites."

The lad standing opposite chuckled understandingly and the capitalist continued to puff at his cigar.

"Spring was the best time," observed he after a moment, "to steal off after the plowing and planting were done and wade up some brook———"

"Where the water foamed over the rocks," interrupted the boy, with sparkling eyes. "We had a brook behind our house. There were great flat rocks in it and further up in the woods some fine, deep trout holes. All you had to do was to toss a line in there and the next you knew———"

"Something would jump for it," cried the millionaire, breaking in turn into the conversation and rubbing his hands. "I remember hauling a two-pounder out of just such a spot. Jove, but he was a fighter! I can see him now, thrashing about in the water. I wasn't equipped with a rod of split bamboo, a reel, and scores of flies in those days. A hook, a worm, and a stick you'd cut yourself was your outfit. Nevertheless I managed to land my fish for all that."

Lured by the subject Ted came nearer.

"Any pickerel holes where you lived?" inquired Mr. Fernald boyishly.

"You bet there were!" replied the lad. "We had a black, scraggy pond two miles away, dotted with stumps and rotting tree trunks. About sundown we fellows would steal a leaky old punt anchored there and pole along the water's edge until we reached a place where the water was deep, and then we'd toss a line in among the roots. It wasn't long before there would be something doing," concluded he, with a merry laugh.

"How gamey those fish are!" observed Mr. Fernald reminiscently. "And bass are sporty, too."

"I'd rather fish for bass than anything else!" asserted Ted.

"Ever tried landlocked salmon?"

"N—o. We didn't get those."

"That's what you get in Maine and New Brunswick," explained Mr. Fernald. "I don't know, though, that they are any more fun to land than a good, spirited bass. I often think that all these fashionable camps with their guides, and canoes, and fishing tackles of the latest variety can't touch a Vermont brook just after the ice has thawed. I'd give all I own to live one of those days of my boyhood over again!"

"So would I!" echoed Ted.

"Pooh, nonsense!" objected Mr. Fernald. "You are young and will probably scramble over the rocks for years to come. But I'm an old chap, too stiff in the joints now to wade a brook. Still it is a pleasure to go back to it in your mind."

His face became grave, then lighted with a quick smile.

"I'll wager the material for those curtains of yours never was bought round here. Didn't that come from Vermont? And the andirons, too?"

"Yes, sir."

"Ah, I knew it! We had some of that old shiny chintz at home for curtains round my mother's four-poster bed."

He rose and began to pace the room thoughtfully.

"Some day my son is going to bring his boy over here," he remarked. "He is interested in electricity and knows quite a bit about it. I was always attracted to science when I was a youngster. I——"

He got no further for there was a stir outside, a sound of voices, and a snapping of dry twigs; and as Ted glanced through the broad frame of the doorway he saw to his amazement Mr. Clarence Fernald wheel up the incline just outside a rubber-tired chair in which sat Laurie.

"I declare if here isn't my grandson now!" exclaimed Mr. Fernald, bustling toward the entrance of the shack.

Ah, it needed no great perception on Ted's part to interpret the pride, affection, and eagerness of the words; in the tones of the elder man's voice rang echoes of adoration, hope, fear, and disappointment. The millowner, however, speedily put them all to rout by crying heartily:

"Well, well! This seems to be a Fernald reunion!"

"Grandfather! Are you here?" cried the boy in the chair, extending his thin hand with the vivid smile Ted so well remembered.

"Indeed I am! Young Turner and I were just speaking of you. I told him you were coming to see him some day."

Laurie glanced toward Ted.

"It is nice of you to let me come and visit you," he said, with easy friendliness. "What a pretty place you have and how gay the flowers are! And the river is beautiful! Our view of it from Pine Lea is not half so lovely as this."

"Perhaps you might like to sit here on the platform for a while," suggested Ted, coming forward rather shyly and smiling down into the lad's eyes. Laurie returned the smile with delightful candor.

"You're Ted Turner, aren't you?" inquired he. "They've told me about you and how many things you can do. I could not rest until I had seen the shack. Besides, Dad says you have some books on electricity; I want to see them. And I've brought you some of mine. They're in a package somewhere under my feet."

"That was mighty kind of you," answered Ted, as he stooped to secure the volumes.

"Not a bit. My tutor, Mr. Hazen, got them for me and some of them are corking—not at all dry and stupid as books often are. If you haven't seen them already, I know you'll like them."

How easily and naturally it all came about! Before they knew it, Mr. Fernald was talking, Mr. Clarence Fernald was talking, Laurie was talking, and Ted himself was talking. Sitting there so idly in the sunshine they joked, told stories, and watched the river as it crept lazily along, reflecting on its smooth surface the gold and azure of the June day. During the pauses they listened to the whispering music of the pines and drank in their sleepy fragrance. More than once Ted pinched himself to make certain that he was really awake. It all seemed so unbelievable; and yet, withal, there was something so simple and suitable about it.

By and by Mr. Clarence rose, stretched his arms, and began boyishly to skip stones across the stream; then Ted tried his skill; and presently, not to be outdone by the others, Grandfather Fernald cast aside his dignity and peeling off his coat joined in the sport.

How Laurie laughed, and how he clapped his hands when one of his grandfather's pebbles skimmed the surface of the water six times before it disappeared amid a series of widening ripples. After this they all were simply boys together, calling, shouting, and jesting with one another in good-humored rivalry. What use was it then ever again to attempt to be austere and unapproachable Fernalds? No use in the world!

Although Mr. Fernald, senior, mopped his brow and slipped back into his coat with a shadow of surprise when he came to and realized what he had been doing, he did not seem to mind greatly having lapsed from seventy years to seven. The fact that he had furnished Laurie with amusement was worth a certain loss of dignity.

Ah, it would have taken an outsider days, weeks, months, perhaps years to have broken through the conventionalities and beheld the Fernalds as Ted saw them that day. It was the magic of the sunshine, the sparkle of the creeping river, the mysterious spell of the pines that had wrought the enchantment. Perhaps, too, the memory of his Vermont boyhood had risen freshly to Grandfather Fernald's mind.

When the shadows lengthened and the glint of gold faded from the river, they went indoors and Mr. Laurie was wheeled about that he might inspect every corner of the little house of which he had heard so much. This he did with the keenest delight and it was only after both his father and his grandfather had promised to bring him again that he could be persuaded to be carried back to Pine Lea. As he disappeared among the windings of the trees, he waved his hand to Ted and called:

"I'll see you some day next week, Ted. Mr. Hazen, my tutor, shall bring me round here some afternoon when you have finished work. I suppose you don't get through much before five, do you?"

"No, I don't."

"Oh, any time you want to see Ted I guess he can be let off early," cried both Mr. Fernald and Mr. Clarence in one breath.

Then as Mr. Clarence pushed the wheel-chair farther into the dusk of the pines, Mr. Fernald turned toward Ted and added in an undertone:

"It's done the lad good to come. I haven't seen him in such high spirits for days. We'll fix things up with Wharton so that whenever he fancies to come here you can be on hand. The poor boy hasn't many pleasures and he sees few persons of his own age."

CHAPTER VII

MR. LAURIE

The visits of Laurie during the following two weeks became very frequent; and such pleasure did they afford him that orders were issued for Ted Turner to knock off work each day at four o'clock and return to the shack, where almost invariably he found his new acquaintance awaiting him. It was long since Laurie Fernald had had a person of his own age to talk with. In fact, he had never before seen a lad whose friendship he desired. Most boys were so well and strong that they had no conception of what it meant not to be so, and their very robustness and vitality overwhelmed a personality as sensitively attuned as was that of Laurie Fernald. He shrank from their pity, their blundering sympathy, their patronage.

But in Ted Turner he immediately felt he had nothing to dread. He might have been a Marathon athlete, so far as any hint to the contrary went. Ted appeared never to notice his disability or to be conscious of any difference in their physical equipment; and when, as sometimes happened, he stooped to arrange a pillow, or lift the wheel-chair over the threshold, he did it so gently and yet in such a matter-of-fact manner that one scarcely noticed it. They were simply eager, alert, bubbling, interested boys together, and as the effect of the friendship showed itself in Laurie's shining eyes, all the Fernalds encouraged it.

"Why, that young Turner is doing Laurie more good than a dozen doctors!" asserted Grandfather Fernald. "If he did no work on the farm at all, Ted would be worth his wages. Money can't pay for what he has done already. I'm afraid Laurie has been missing young friends more than we realized. He never complains and perhaps we did not suspect how lonely he was."

Mr. Clarence nodded.

"Older people are pretty stupid about children sometimes, I guess," said he sadly. "Well, he has Ted Turner now and certainly he is a splendid boy for him to be with. Laurie's tutor, Mr. Hazen, likes him tremendously. What a blessing it is that Wharton stumbled on him and brought him up here. Had we searched the countryside I doubt if we could have found any one Laurie would have liked so much. He doesn't care especially for strangers."

With the Fernald's sanction behind the friendship, and both Laurie's tutor and his doctor urging it on, you may be sure it thrived vigorously. The boys were naturally companionable and now, with every barrier out of the way, and every fostering influence provided, the two soon found themselves on terms of genuine affection.

If Laurie went for a motor ride Saturday afternoon, Ted must go, too; if he had a new book, Ted must share it, and when he was not as well as usual, or it was too stormy for him to be carried to the shack, nothing would do but Ted Turner must be summoned to Pine Lea to brighten the dreariness of the day. Soon the servants came to know the newcomer and understand that he was a privileged person in the household. Laurie's mother, a pretty Southern woman, welcomed him kindly and it was not long before the two were united in a deep and affectionate conspiracy which placed them on terms of the greatest intimacy.

"Laurie isn't quite so well this afternoon, Ted," Mrs. Fernald would say. "Don't let him get too excited or talk too much." Or sometimes it was, "Laurie had a bad night last night and is dreadfully discouraged to-day. Do try and cheer him up."

Not infrequently Mr. Hazen would voice an appeal:

"I haven't been able to coax Laurie to touch his French lesson this morning. Don't you want to see if you can't get him started on it? He'll do anything for you."

And when Ted did succeed in getting the lesson learned, and not only that but actually made an amusing game out of it, how grateful Mr. Hazen was!

For with all his sweetness Laurie Fernald had a stubborn streak in his nature which the volume of attention he had received had only served to accentuate. He was not really spoiled but there were times when he would do as he pleased, whether or no; and when such a mood came to the surface, no one but Ted Turner seemed to have any power against it. Therefore, when it occasionally chanced that Laurie refused to see the doctor, or would not take his medicine, or insisted on getting up when told to lie in bed, Ted was made an ally and urged to promote the thing that made for the invalid's health and well-being.

After being admitted into the family circle on such confidential terms, it followed that absolute equality was accorded Ted and he came and went freely, both at Aldercliffe and Pine Lea. He read with Laurie, lunched with him, followed his lessons; and listened to his plans, his pleasures, and his disappointments. Perhaps, too, Laurie Fernald liked and respected him the more that he had duties to perform and therefore was not always free to come at his beck and call as did everybody else.

"I shan't be able to get round to see you to-day, old chap," Ted would explain over the telephone. "There is a second crop of peas to plant in the further lot and as Mr. Stevens is short of men, I'm going to duff in and help, even if it isn't my job. Of course I want to do my bit when they are in a pinch. I'll see you to-morrow."

And although Laurie grumbled a good deal, he recognized the present need, and becoming interested in the matter in spite of himself, wished to hear the following day all about the planting. That he should inquire greatly delighted both his father and his grandfather who had always been anxious that he should come into touch with the management of the estates. Often they had tried to talk to him of crops and gardens, plowing and planting, but to the subject the heir had lent merely a deaf ear. Now with Ted Turner's advent had come a new influence, the testimony of one who was practically interested in agricultural problems and thought farming anything but dull. The boy was genuinely eager that the work of the men should be a success and therefore when he hoped for fair weather for the haying and it seemed to make a real difference to him whether it was pleasant or not, how could Laurie help being eager that it should not rain until the fields were mowed and the crop garnered into the great barns? Or when Ted was worrying about the pests that invaded the garden, one wouldn't have been a true friend not to ask how the warfare was progressing.

Before Laurie knew it, he had learned much about the affairs of the estates and had become awake to the obstacles good farmers encounter in their strife with soil and weather conditions. As a result his outlook broadened, he became less introspective and more alive to the concerns of those about him; and he gained a new respect for his father's and grandfather's employees. One had much less time to be depressed and discouraged when one had so many things to think of.

Sometimes Ted brought in seeds and showed them; and afterward a slender plant that had sprouted; and then Mr. Hazen would join in and tell the two boys of other plants,—strange ones that grew in novel ways. Or perhaps the talk led to the chemicals the gardeners were mixing with the soil and wandered off into science. Every topic seemed to reach so far and led into such fascinating mazes of knowledge! What a surprising place the world was!

Of course, had the Fernalds so desired they could have relieved Ted of all his farming duties, and indeed they were sorely tempted at times to do so; but when they saw how much better it was to keep the boy's visits a novelty instead of making of them a commonplace event, and sensed how much knowledge he was bringing into the invalid's room, they decided to let matters progress as they were going. They did, however, arrange occasional holidays for the lad and many a jolly outing did Ted have in consequence. Had they displayed less wisdom they might have wrecked the friendship altogether. As it was they strengthened it daily and the little shack among the pines became to both Ted and to Laurie the most loved spot in the world. Frequently the servants from Pine Lea surprised the boys by bringing them their luncheon there; and sometimes Mrs. Fernald herself came hither with her tea-basket, and the entire family sat about before the great stone fireplace and enjoyed a picnic supper.

It was after one of these camping teas that Mr. Clarence Fernald bought for Laurie a comfortable Adirondack canoe luxuriously fitted up with cushions. The stream before the boathouse was broad and contained little or no current except down toward Pine Lea, where it narrowed into rapids that swept over the dam at Freeman's Falls. Therefore if one kept along the edges of the upper part of the river, there was no danger and the canoe afforded a delightful recreation. Both the elder Fernalds and Mr. Hazen rowed well and Ted pulled an exceptionally strong oar for a boy of his years. Hence they took turns at propelling the boat and soon Laurie was as much at home on the pillows in the stern as he was in his wheel-chair.

He greatly enjoyed the smooth, jarless motion of the craft; and often, even when it was anchored at the float, he liked to be lifted into it and lie there rocking with the wash of the river. It made a change which he declared rested him, and it was through this simple and apparently harmless pleasure that a terrible catastrophe took place.

On a fine warm afternoon Mr. Hazen and Laurie went over to the shack to meet Ted who usually returned from work shortly after four o'clock. The door of the little camp was wide open when they arrived but their host was nowhere to be seen. This circumstance did not trouble them, however, for on the days when Laurie was expected Ted always left the boathouse unlocked. What did disconcert them and make Laurie impatient was to discover that through some error in reckoning they were almost an hour too early.

"Our clocks must have been ahead of time," fretted the boy. "We shall have to hang round here the deuce of a while."

"Wouldn't you like me to wheel you back through the grove?" questioned the tutor.

"Oh, there's no use in that. Suppose you get out the pillows and help me into the boat. I'll lie there a while and rest."

"All right."

With a ready smile Mr. Hazen plunged into the shack and soon returned laden with the crimson cushions, which he arranged in the stern of the canoe with greatest care. Afterward he picked Laurie up in his arms as if he had been a feather and carried him to the boat.

"How's that?" he asked, when the invalid was settled.

"Fine! Great, thanks! You're a wonder with pillows, Mr. Hazen; you always get them just right," replied the lad. "Now if I only had my book——"

"I could go and get it."

"Oh, no. Don't bother. Ted will be here before long, won't he? What time is it?"

"About half-past three."

"Only half-past three! Great Scott! I thought it must be nearly four by this time. Then I have quite a while to wait, don't I? I don't see why you got me over here so early."

"I don't either," returned Mr. Hazen pleasantly. "I'm afraid my watch must have been wrong."

Laurie moved restlessly on the pillows. He had passed a wretched night and was worn and nervous in consequence.

"I guess perhaps you'd better run back to the house for my book," remarked he presently. "I shall be having a fit of the blues if I have to hang round here so long with nothing to do."

"I'm perfectly willing to go back," Mr. Hazen said. "But are you sure——"

"Oh, I'm all right," cut in the boy sharply. "I guess I can sit in a boat by myself for a little while."

"Still, I'm not certain that I ought to——"

"Leave me? Nonsense! What do you think I am, Hazen? A baby? What on earth is going to happen to me, I'd like to know?"

"Nevertheless I don't like to——"

"Oh, do stop arguing. It makes me tired. Cut along and get the book, can't you? Why waste all this time fussing?" burst out the invalid fretfully. "How am I ever going to get well, or think

I am well, if you keep reminding me every minute that I am a helpless wreck? It is enough to discourage anybody. Why can't you treat me like other people? If you chose to sit in a boat alone for half an hour nobody'd throw a fit. Why can't I?"

"I suppose you can," retorted the tutor unwillingly. "Only you know we never do——"

"Leave me? Don't I know it? The way people tag at my heels drives me almost crazy sometimes. You wouldn't like to have some one dogging your footsteps from morning until night, would you?"

"I'm afraid I shouldn't," admitted Mr. Hazen.

For an interval Laurie was silent; then he glanced up with one of his swift, appealing smiles.

"There, there, Mr. Hazen!" he said with winning sincerity. "Forgive me. I didn't mean to be cross. I do get so fiendishly impatient sometimes. How you can keep on being so kind to me I don't see. Do please go and get the book, like a good chap. It's on the chair in my room or else on the library table. You'll find it somewhere. 'Treasure Island,' you know. I had to leave it in the middle of a most exciting chapter and I am crazy to know how it came out."

Reluctantly Mr. Hazen moved away. It was very hard to resist Laurie Fernald when he was in his present mood; besides, the young tutor was genuinely fond of his charge and would far rather gratify his wishes than refuse him anything. Therefore he hurried off through the grove, resolving to return as fast as ever he could.

In the meantime Laurie threw his head back on the pillows and looked up at the sky. How blue it was and how lazily the clouds drifted by! Was any spot on earth so still as this? Why, you could not hear a sound! He yawned and closed his eyes, the fatigue of his sleepless night overcoming him. Soon he was lost in dreams.

He never could tell just what it was that aroused him; perhaps it was a premonition of danger, perhaps the rocking of the boat. At any rate he was suddenly broad awake to find himself drifting out into the middle of the stream. In some way the boat must have become unfastened and the rising breeze carried it away from shore. Not that it mattered very much now. The thing that was of consequence was that he was helplessly drifting down the river with no means of staying his progress. Soon he would be caught in the swirl of the current and then there would be no help for him. What was he to do?

Must he lie there and be borne along until he was at last carried over the dam at his father's mills?

He saw no escape from such a fate! There was not a soul in sight. The banks of the river were entirely deserted, for the workmen were far away, toiling in the fields and gardens, and they could not hear him even were he to shout his loudest. As for Mr. Hazen, he was probably still at Pine Lea searching for the book and wouldn't be back for some time.

The boy's heart sank and he quivered with fear. Must he be drowned there all alone? Was there no one to aid him?

Thoroughly terrified, he began to scream. But his screams only reëchoed from the silent river banks. No one heard and no one came.

He was in the current of the stream now and moving rapidly along. Faster and faster he went. Yes, he was going to be swept on to Freeman's Falls, going to be carried over the dam and submerged beneath that hideous roar of water that foamed down on the jagged rocks in a boiling torrent of noise and spray. Nobody would know his plight until the catastrophe was over;

He heard an answering shout and a second later
saw Ted Turner dash through the pines.

and even should any of the mill hands catch sight of his frail craft as it sped past it would be too late for them to help him. Before a boat could be launched and rescuers summoned he would be over the falls.

Yes, he was going to die, *to die!*

Again he screamed, this time less with a thought of calling for help than as a protest against the fate awaiting him. To his surprise he heard an answering shout and a second later saw Ted Turner dash through the pines, pause on the shore, and scan the stream. Another instant and the boy had thrown off his coat and shoes and was in the water, swimming toward the boat with quick, overhand strokes.

"Keep perfectly still, Laurie!" he panted. "You're all right. Just don't get fussed."

Yet cheering as were the words, they could not conceal the fact that Ted was frightened, terribly frightened.

The canoe gained headway with the increasing current. It seemed now to leap along. And in just the proportion that its progress was accelerated, the speed of the pursuer lessened. It seemed as if Ted would never overtake his prize. How they raced one another, the bobbing craft and the breathless boy! Ted Turner was a strong swimmer but the canoe with its solitary occupant was so light that it shot over the surface of the water like a feather.

Was the contest to be a losing one, after all?

Laurie, looking back at the wake of the boat, saw Ted's arm move slower and slower and suddenly a wave of realization of the other's danger came upon him. They might both be drowned,—two of them instead of one!

"Give it up, old man!" he called bravely. "Don't try any more. You may go down yourself and I should have to die with that misery on my soul. You've done your best. It's all right. Just let me go! I'm not afraid."

There was no answer from the swimmer but he did not stop. On the contrary, he kept stubbornly on, plowing with mechanical persistence through the water. Then at length he, too, was in the current and was gaining surely and speedily. Presently he was only a length away from the boat—he was nearer—nearer! His arm touched the stern and Laurie Fernald caught his hand in a firm grip. There he hung, breathing heavily.

"I've simply got to stop a second or two and get my wind," said he. "Then we'll start back."

"Ted!"

"There are no oars, of course, but I can tie the rope around my body or perhaps catch it between my teeth. The canoe isn't heavy, you know. After we get out of the current and into quiet water, we shall have no trouble. We can cut straight across the stream and the distance to shore won't be great. I can do it all right."

And do it he did, just how neither of the lads could have told. Nevertheless he did contrive to bring the boat and Laurie with it to a place of safety. Shoulder-deep in the water stood the frenzied Mr. Hazen who had plunged in to meet them and drag them to land. They had come so far down the river that when the canoe was finally beached they found themselves opposite the sweeping lawns of Pine Lea.

Ted and the tutor were chilled and exhausted and Laurie was weak from fright and excitement. It did not take long, you may be sure, to summon help and bundle the three into a motor car which carried them to Pine Lea. Once there the invalid was put to bed and Mr. Hazen and Ted equipped with dry garments.

"I shall get the deuce from the Fernalds for this!" commented the young tutor gloomily to Ted. "If it had not been for you, that boy would certainly have been drowned. Ugh! It makes me shudder to think of it! Had anything happened to him, I believe his father and grandfather would have lynched me."

"Oh, Laurie is going to take all the blame," replied Ted, making an attempt to comfort the dejected young man. "He told me so himself."

"That's all very well," rejoined Mr. Hazen, "but it won't help much. I shouldn't have left him. I had no right to do it, no matter what he said. I suppose the boat wasn't securely tied. It couldn't have been. Then the breeze came up. Goodness knows how the thing actually happened. I can't understand it now. But the point is, it did. Jove! I'm weak as a rag! I guess there can't be much left of you, Ted."

"Oh, I'm all right now," protested Ted. "What got me was the fright of it. I didn't mind the swimming, for I've often crossed the river and back during my morning plunge. My work keeps me in pretty good training. But to-day I got panicky and my breath gave out. I was so afraid I wouldn't overtake the boat before——"

"I know!" interrupted the tutor with a shiver. "Well, it is all over now, thank God! You were a genuine hero and I shall tell the Fernalds so."

"Stuff! Don't tell them at all. What's the use of harrowing their feelings all up now that the thing is past and done with?"

"But Laurie—he is all done up and they will be at a loss to account for it," objected Mr. Hazen. "Besides, the servants saw us come ashore and have probably already spread the story all over the place. And anyhow, I believe in being perfectly aboveboard. You do yourself, you know that. So I shall tell them the whole thing precisely as it happened. Afterward they'll probably fire me."

"No, they won't! Cheer up!"

"I deserve to be fired, too," went on the young tutor without heeding the interruption. "I ought not to have left Laurie an instant."

"Perhaps not. But you won't do it again."

"You bet I won't!" cried Mr. Hazen boyishly.

It subsequently proved that Mr. Hazen knew far more of his employers than did Ted, for after the story was told only the pleas of the young rescuer availed to soften the sentence imposed.

"He's almighty sorry, Mr. Fernald," asserted Ted Turner. "Don't tip him out. Give him a second try. He won't ever do it again."

"W—e—ll, for your sake I will," Mr. Clarence said, yielding reluctantly to the pleading of the lad who sat opposite. "It would be hard for me to deny you anything after what you've done. You've saved our boy's life. We never shall forget it, never. But Hazen can thank you for his job—not me."

And so, as a result of Ted's intercession, Mr. Hazen stayed on. In fact, as Mr. Clarence said, they could deny the lad nothing. It seemed as if the Fernalds never could do enough for him. Grandfather Fernald gave him a new watch with an illuminated face; and quite unknown to any one, Laurie's father opened a bank account to his credit, depositing a substantial sum as a "starter."

But the best of the whole thing was that Laurie turned to Ted with a deeper and more earnest affection and the foundation was laid for a strong and enduring friendship.

CHAPTER VIII

DIPLOMACY AND ITS RESULTS

Laurie, Ted, and Mr. Hazen were in the shack on a Saturday afternoon not long after the adventure on the river. A hard shower had driven them ashore and forced them to scramble into the shelter of the camp at the water's edge. How the rain pelted down on the low roof! It seemed as if an army were bombarding the little hut! Within doors, however, all was tight, warm, and cosy and on the hearth before a roaring fire the damp coats were drying.

In the meantime the two boys and the young tutor had dragged out some coils of wire and a pair of amateur telephone transmitters which Ted had concocted while in school and for amusement were trying to run from one end of the room to the other a miniature telephone. Thus far their attempts had not been successful and Ted was becoming impatient.

"We got quite a fair result at the laboratory after the things were adjusted," commented he. "I don't see why we can't work the same stunt here."

"I'm afraid we haven't put time enough into it yet," replied Mr. Hazen. "Don't you remember how long Alexander Graham Bell, the inventor of the telephone, experimented before he got results?"

Laurie, who was busy shortening a bit of wire, glanced up with interest.

"I can't for the life of me understand how he knew what he wanted to do, can you?" he mused. "Think of starting out to make something perfectly new—a machine for which you had no pattern! I can imagine working out improvements on something already on the market. But to produce something nobody had ever seen before—that beats me! How did he ever get the idea in the first place?"

The tutor smiled.

"Mr. Bell did not set out to make a telephone, Laurie," he answered. "What he was aiming to do was to perfect a harmonic telegraph, a scheme to which he had been devoting a good deal of his time. He and his father had studied carefully the miracle of speech—how the sounds of the human voice were produced and carried to others—and as a result of this training Mr. Bell had become an expert teacher of the deaf. He was also professor of Vocal Physiology at Boston University where he had courses in lip reading, or a system of visible speech, which his father had evolved. This work kept him busy through the day so whatever experimenting he did with sounds and their vibrations had to be done at night."

"So he stole time for electrical work, too, did he?" observed Ted.

"I'm afraid that his interest in sound vibration caused him a sorry loss of sleep," said the tutor. "But certainly his later results were worth the amount of rest he sacrificed. One of the first agencies he employed to work upon was a piano. Have you ever tried singing a note into this instrument when the sustaining pedal is depressed? Do it some time and notice what happens. You will find that the string tuned to the pitch of your voice will start vibrating while all the others remain quiet. You can even go farther and try the experiment of uttering several different pitches, if you want to, and the corresponding strings will give back your notes, each one singling out its own particular vibration from the air. Now the results reached in these experiments with the piano strings meant a great deal more to Alexander Graham Bell than they would have meant to you or to me. In the first place, his training had given him a very acute ear; and in the next place, he was able to see in the facts presented a significance which an unskilled listener would not have detected. He found that this law of sympathetic vibration could be repeated electrically and, if desired, from a distance by means of electromagnets placed under a group of piano strings; and if afterward a circuit was made by connecting the magnets with an electric battery, you immediately had the same singing of the keys and a similar searching of each for its own pitch."

"I'd like to try that trick some time," exclaimed Ted, leaning forward eagerly.

"So should I!" echoed Laurie.

"I think we could quite easily make the experiment if Laurie's mother would not object to our rigging up an attachment to her piano," Mr. Hazen responded.

"Oh, Mater wouldn't mind," answered Laurie confidently. "She never minds anything I want to do."

"I know she is a very long-suffering person," smiled the tutor. "Do you recall the white mice you had once, Laurie, and how they got loose and ran all over the house?"

"And the chameleons! And the baby alligator!" chuckled Laurie. "Mother did get her back up over that alligator. She didn't like meeting him in the hall unexpectedly. But she wouldn't mind a thing that wasn't alive."

"You call an electric wire dead then," said Ted with irony.

"Well, no—not precisely," grinned Laurie. "Still I'm certain

Mater would be less scared of it than she would of a mouse, even if the wire could kill her and the mouse couldn't."

"Let's return to Mr. Bell and his piano strings," Ted remarked, after the laughter had subsided.

Mr. Hazen's brow contracted thoughtfully and in his leisurely fashion he presently replied:

"You can see, can't you, that if an interrupter caused the electric current to be made and broken at intervals, the number of times it interrupted per second would, for example, correspond to the rate of vibration in one of the strings? In other words, that would be the only string that would answer. Now if you sang into the piano, you would have the rhythmic impulse that set the piano strings vibrating coming directly through the air, while with the battery the impulse would come through the wire and the electromagnets instead. In each case, however, the principle involved would be the same."

"I can see that," said Ted quickly. "Can't you, Laurie?"

His chum nodded.

"Now," continued Mr. Hazen, "just as it was possible to start two or more different notes of the piano echoing varying pitches, so it is possible to have several sets of these *make-and-break* or intermittent currents start their corresponding strings to answering. In this way one could send several messages at once, each message being toned to a different pitch. All that would be necessary would be to have differently keyed interrupters. This was the principle of the harmonic telegraph at which Mr. Bell was toiling outside the hours of his regular work and through which he hoped to make himself rich and famous. His intention was to break up the various sounds into the dots and dashes of the Morse code and make one wire do what it had previously taken several wires to perform."

"It seems simple enough," speculated Laurie.

"It was not so simple to carry out," declared Mr. Hazen. "Of course, as I told you, Mr. Bell could not give his entire time to it. He had his teaching both at Boston University and elsewhere to do. Nor was he wholly free at the Saunders's, with whom he boarded at Salem, for he was helping the Saunders's nephew, who was deaf, to study."

"And in return poor Mrs. Saunders had to offer up her piano for experiments, I suppose," Ted observed.

"Well, perhaps at first—but not for long," was Mr. Hazen's reply. "Mr. Bell soon abandoned piano strings and in their place resorted to flat strips of springy steel, keying them to different pitches by varying their length. One end of these strips he fastened to a pole of an electromagnet and the other he extended over the other pole and left free."

"And the current interrupters?" queried Ted.

"Those current interrupters are the things which have since become known as transmitters," explained Mr. Hazen. "Those Mr. Bell made all alike except that in each one of them were springs kept in constant vibration by a magnet or point of metal placed above each spring so that the spring would touch it at every vibration, thus making and breaking the electric current the same number of times per second that corresponded to the pitch of the piece of steel. By tuning the springs of the receivers to the same pitch with the transmitters and running a wire between them equipped with signalling keys and a battery, Bell reasoned he could send as many messages at one time as there were pitches."

"Did he get it to work?" Laurie asked.

"Mr. Bell didn't, no," replied the tutor. "What sounded logical enough on paper was not so easy to put into practise. The idea has been carried out successfully, however, since then. But Mr. Bell unfortunately had no end of troubles with his scheme, and we all may thank these difficulties for the telephone, for had his harmonic telegraph gone smoothly we might not and probably would not have had Bell's other and far more important invention."

"The discovery of the telephone was a 'happen,' then," Ted ventured.

"More or less of a happen," was the reply. "Of course, the intelligent recognition of the law behind it was not a happen; nor was the patient and persistent toil that went into the perfecting of the instrument a matter of chance. Alexander Graham Bell had the genius to recognize the value and significance of the truth on which he stumbled and turn it to practical purposes. Many another might perhaps have heard the self-same sounds that came to him over that reach of wire and, detecting nothing unusual in the whining vibrations, have passed them by. But to Mr. Bell they were magic music, the sesame to a new country. Strangely enough, too, it was the good luck of a boy not much older than Ted to share with the discoverer the wonderful secret."

"How?" demanded both Laurie and Ted in a breath.

"I can't tell you that story to-day," Mr. Hazen expostulated. "It would take much too long. We must give over talking and put our minds on this telephone of our own which does not seem to be making any great progress. I begin to be afraid we haven't the proper outfit."

As he spoke, a shadow crossed the window and in another instant Mr. Clarence Fernald poked his head in at the door.

"What are you three conspirators up to?" inquired he. "You look as if you were making bombs or some other deadly thing."

"We are making a telephone, Dad, and it won't work," was Laurie's answer.

Mr. Fernald smiled with amusement.

"You seem to have plenty of wire," he said. "In fact, if I were permitted to offer a criticism, I should say you had more wire than anything else. How lengthy a circuit do you expect to cover?"

"Oh, we're not ambitious," Laurie replied. "If we can cross the room we shall be satisfied, although now that you mention it, perhaps it wouldn't be such a bad thing if it could run from my room at home over here." He eyed his father furtively. "Then when I happened to have to stay in bed I could talk to Ted and he could cheer me up."

"So he could!" echoed Mr. Fernald in noncommittal fashion.

"It would be rather nice, too, for Mr. Wharton," went on the diplomat with his sidelong glance still fixed on his father. "He must sometimes wish he could reach Ted without bothering to send a man way over here. And then there are the Turners! Of course a telephone to the shack would give them no end of pleasure. They must miss Ted and often want to speak with him."

He waited but there was no response from Mr. Fernald.

"Ted might be sick, too; or have an accident and wish to get help and——"

At last the speaker was rewarded by having the elder man turn quickly upon him.

"In other words, you young scoundrel, you want me to install a telephone in this shack for the joy and delight of you two electricians who can't seem to do it for yourselves," said Mr. Fernald gruffly.

"Now however do you suppose he guessed it?" exclaimed

Laurie delightedly, as he turned with mock gravity to Ted. "Isn't he the mind reader?"

It was evident that Laurie Fernald thoroughly understood his father and that the two were on terms of the greatest affection.

"Did I say I wanted a telephone?" he went on meekly.

"You said everything else," was the grim retort.

"Did I? Well, well!" commented the boy mischievously. "I needn't have taken so much trouble after all, need I? But every one isn't such a Sherlock Holmes as you are, Dad."

Mr. Fernald's scowl vanished and he laughed.

"What a young wheedler you are!" observed he, playfully rumpling up his son's fair hair. "You could coax every cent I have away from me if I did not lock my money up in the bank. I really think, though, that a telephone here in the hut would be an excellent idea. But what I don't see is why you don't do the job yourselves."

"Oh, we could do the work all right if there wasn't danger of our infringing the patent of the telephone company," was Laurie's impish reply. "If we should get into a lawsuit there would be no end of trouble, you know. I guess we'd much better have the thing installed in the regular way."

"I guess so too!" came from his father.

"You'll really have it put in, Dad?" cried Laurie.

"Sure!"

"That will be bully, corking!" Laurie declared. "You're mighty good, Dad."

"Pooh! Nonsense!" his father protested, as he shot a quick glance of tenderness toward the boy. "A telephone over here will be a useful thing for us all. I may want to call Ted up myself sometimes. We never can tell when an emergency may arise."

Within the following week the telephone was in place and

although Ted had not minded his seclusion, or thought he had not, he suddenly found that the instrument gave him a very comfortable sense of nearness to his family and to the household at Pine Lea. He and Laurie chattered like magpies over the wire and were far worse, Mrs. Fernald asserted, than any two gossipy boarding-school girls. Moreover, Ted was now able to speak each day with his father at the Fernald shipping rooms and by this means keep in closer touch with his family. As for Mr. Wharton, he marvelled that a telephone to the shack had not been put in at the outset.

"It is not a luxury," he insisted. "It's a necessity! An indispensable part of the farm equipment!"

Certainly in the days to come it proved its worth!

CHAPTER IX

THE STORY OF THE FIRST TELEPHONE

I am going down to Freeman's Falls this afternoon to get some rubber tape," Ted remarked to Laurie, as the two boys and the tutor were eating a picnic lunch in Ted's cabin one Saturday.

"Oh, make somebody else do your errand and stay here," Laurie begged. "Anybody can buy that stuff. Some of the men must be going to the Falls. Ask Wharton to make them do your shopping."

"Perhaps Ted had other things to attend to," ventured Mr. Hazen.

"No, I hadn't," was the prompt reply.

"In that case I am sure any of the men would be glad to get whatever you please," the tutor declared.

"Save your energy, old man," put in Laurie. "Electrical supplies are easy enough to buy when you know what you want."

"They are now," Mr. Hazen remarked, with a quiet smile, "but they have not always been. In fact, it was not so very long ago that it was almost impossible to purchase either books on electricity or electrical stuff of any sort. People's knowledge of such matters was so scanty that little was written about them; and as for shops of this type—why, they were practically unknown."

"Where did persons get what they wanted?" asked Ted with surprise.

"Nobody wanted electrical materials," laughed Mr. Hazen. "There was no call for them. Even had the shops supplied them, nobody would have known what to do with them."

"But there must have been some who would," the boy persisted. "Where, for example, did Mr. Bell get his things?"

"Practically all Mr. Bell's work was done at a little shop on Court Street, Boston," answered Mr. Hazen. "This shop, however, was nothing like the electrical supply shops we have now. Had Alexander Graham Bell entered its doors and asked, for instance, for a telephone transmitter, he would have found no such thing in stock. On the contrary, the shop consisted of a number of benches where men or boys experimented or made crude electrical contrivances that had previously been ordered by customers. The shop was owned by Charles Williams, a clever mechanical man, who was deeply interested in electrical problems of all sorts. In a tiny showcase in the front part of the store were displayed what few textbooks on electricity he had been able to gather together and these he allowed the men in his employ to read at lunch time and to use freely in connection with their work. He was a person greatly beloved by those associated with him and he had the rare wisdom to leave every man he employed unhampered, thereby making individual initiative the law of his business."

The tutor paused, then noticing that both the boys were listening intently, he continued:

"If a man had an idea that had been carefully thought out, he was given free rein to execute it. Tom Watson, one of the boys at the shop, constructed a miniature electric engine, and although the feat took both time and material, there was no quarrel because of that. The place was literally a workshop, and so long as there were no drones in it and the men toiled intelligently, Mr. Williams had no fault to find. You can imagine what valuable training such a practical environment furnished. Nobody nagged at the men, nobody drove them on. Each of the thirty or forty employees pegged away at his particular task, either doing work for a specific customer or trying to perfect some notion of his own. If you were a person of ideas, it was an ideal conservatory in which to foster them."

"Gee! I'd have liked the chance to work in a place like that!" Ted sighed.

"It would not have been a bad starter, I assure you," agreed Mr. Hazen. "At that time there were, as I told you, few such shops in the country; and this one, simple and crude as it was, was one of the largest. There was another in Chicago which was bigger and perhaps more perfectly organized; but Williams's shop was about as good as any and certainly gave its men an excellent all-round education in electrical matters. Many of them went out later and became leaders in the rapidly growing world of science and these few historic little shops thus became the ancestors of our vast electrical plants."

"It seems funny to think it all started from such small beginnings, doesn't it," mused Laurie thoughtfully.

"It certainly is interesting," Mr. Hazen replied. "And if it interests us in this far-away time, think what it must have meant to the pioneers to witness the marvels half a century brought forth and look back over the trail they had blazed. For it was a golden era of discovery, that period when the new-born power of electricity made its appearance; and because Williams's shop was known to be a nursery for ideas, into it flocked every variety of dreamer. There were those who dreamed epoch-making dreams and eventually made them come true; and there were those who merely saw visions too impractical ever to become realities. To work amid this mecca of minds must have been not only an education in science but in human nature as well. Every sort of crank who had gathered a wild notion out of the blue meandered into Williams's shop in the hope that somebody could be found there who would provide either the money or the labor to further his particular scheme.

"Now in this shop," went on Mr. Hazen, "there was, as I told you, a young neophyte by the name of Thomas Watson. Tom had not found his niche in life. He had tried being a clerk, a book-keeper, and a carpenter and none of these several occupations had seemed to fit him. Then one fortunate day he happened in at Williams's shop and immediately he knew this was the place where he belonged. He was a boy of mechanical tastes who had a real genius for tools and machinery. He was given a chance to turn castings by hand at five dollars a week and he took the job eagerly."

"Think how a boy would howl at working for that now," Laurie exclaimed.

"No doubt there were boys who would have howled then," answered Mr. Hazen, "although in those days young fellows expected to work hard and receive little pay until they had learned their trade. Perhaps the youthful Mr. Watson had the common sense to cherish this creed; at any rate, there was not a lazy bone in his body, and as there were no such things to be had as automatic screw machines, he went vigorously to work making the castings by hand, trying as he did so not to blind his eyes with the flying splinters of metal."

"Then what happened?" demanded Laurie.

"Well, Watson stuck at his job and in the meantime gleaned right and left such scraps of practical knowledge as a boy would pick up in such a place. By the end of his second year he had

had his finger in many pies and had worked on about every sort of electrical contrivance then known: call bells, annunciators, galvanometers; telegraph keys, sounders, relays, registers, and printing telegraph instruments. Think what a rich experience his two years of apprenticeship had given him!"

"You bet!" ejaculated Ted appreciatively.

"Now as Tom Watson was not only clever but was willing to take infinite pains with whatever he set his hand to, never stinting nor measuring his time or strength, he became a great favorite with those who came to the shop to have different kinds of experimental apparatus made. Many of the ideas brought to him to be worked out came from visionaries who had succeeded in capturing the financial backing of an unwary believer and convinced themselves and him that here was an idea that was to stir the universe. But too many of these schemes, alas, proved worthless and as their common fate was the rubbish heap, it is strange that the indefatigable Thomas Watson did not have his faith in pioneer work entirely destroyed. But youth is buoyed up by perpetual hope; and paradoxical as it may seem, his enthusiasm never lagged. Each time he felt, with the inventor, that they might be standing on the brink of gigantic unfoldings and he toiled with energy to bring something practical out of the chaos. And when at length it became evident beyond all question that the idea was never to unfold into anything practical, he would, with the same zealous spirit, attack another seer's problem."

"Didn't he ever meet any successful inventors?" questioned Ted.

"Yes, indeed," the tutor answered. "Scattered among the cranks and castle builders were several brilliant, solid-headed men. There was Moses G. Farmer, for example, one of the foremost electricians of that time, who had many an excellent and workable idea and who taught young Watson no end of valuable lessons. Then one day into the workshop came Alexander Graham Bell. In his hand he carried a mechanical contrivance Watson had previously made for him and on espying Tom in the distance he made a direct line for the workman's bench. After explaining that the device did not do the thing he was desirous it should, he told Watson that it was the receiver and transmitter of his Harmonic Telegraph."

"And that was the beginning of Mr. Watson's work with Mr. Bell?" asked Ted breathlessly.

"Yes, that was the real beginning."

"Think of working with a man like that!" the boy cried with sparkling eyes. "It must have been tremendously interesting."

"It was interesting," responded Mr. Hazen, "but nevertheless much of the time it must have been inexpressibly tedious work. A young man less patient and persistent than Watson would probably have tired of the task. Just why he did not lose his courage through the six years of struggle that followed I do not understand. For how was he to know but that this idea would eventually prove as hopeless and unprofitable as had so many others to which he had devoted his energy? Beyond Mr. Bell's own magnetic personality there was only slender foundation for his faith, for in spite of the efforts of both men the harmonic telegraph failed to take form. Instead, like a tantalizing sprite, it danced before them, always beckoning, never materializing. In theory it was perfectly consistent but in practise it could not be coaxed into behaving as it logically should. Had it but been possible for those working on it to realize that beyond their temporary failure lay a success glorious past all belief, think what the knowledge would have meant. But to always be following the gleam and never overtaking it, ah, that might well have discouraged prophets of stouter heart!"

"Were these transmitters and receivers made from electro-magnets and strips of flat steel, as you told us the other day?" asked Ted.

"Yes, their essential parts comprised just those elements—an electromagnet and a scrap of flattened clock spring which, as I have explained, was clamped by one end to the pole of the magnet and left free at the other to vibrate over the opposite pole. In addition the transmitter had make-and-break points such as an ordinary telephone bell has, and when these came in contact with the current, the springs inside continually gave out a sort of wail keyed to correspond with the pitch of the spring. As Mr. Bell had six of these instruments tuned to as many different pitches—and six receivers to answer them—you may picture to yourself the hideousness of the sounds amid which the experimenters labored."

"I suppose when each transmitter sent out its particular whine its own similarly tuned receiver spring would wriggle in response," Laurie said.

"Exactly so."

"There must have been lovely music when all six of them began to sing!" laughed Ted.

"Mr. Watson wrote once that it was as if all the miseries of the world were concentrated in that workroom, and I can imagine it being true," answered the tutor. "Well, young Watson certainly did all he could to make the harmonic telegraph a reality. He made the receivers and transmitters exactly as Mr. Bell requested; but on testing them out, great was the surprise of the inventor to find that his idea, so feasible in theory, refused to work. Nevertheless, his faith was not shaken. He insisted on trying to discover the flaw in his logic and correct it, and as Watson had now completed some work that he had been doing for Moses Farmer, the two began a series of experiments that lasted all winter."

"Jove!" ejaculated Laurie.

"Marvels of science are not born in a moment," answered Mr. Hazen. "Yet I do not wonder that you gasp, for think of what it must have meant to toil for weeks and months at those wailing instruments! It is a miracle the men did not go mad. They were not always able to work together for Mr. Bell had his living to earn and therefore was compelled to devote a good measure of his time to his college classes and his deaf pupils. In consequence, he did a portion of his experimental work at Salem while Watson carried on his at the shop, fitting it in with other odd jobs that came his way. Frequently Mr. Bell remained in Boston in the evening and the two worked at the Williams's shop until late into the night."

"Wasn't it lucky there were no labor unions in those days?" put in Ted mischievously.

"Indeed it was!" responded Mr. Hazen. "The shop would then have been barred and bolted at five o'clock, I suppose, and Alexander Graham Bell might have had a million bright ideas for all the good they would have done him. But at that golden period of our history, if an ambitious fellow like Watson wished to put in extra hours of work, the more slothful ones had no authority to stand over him with a club and say he shouldn't. Therefore the young apprentice toiled on with Mr. Bell, unmolested; and Charles Williams, the proprietor of the shop, was perfectly willing he should. One evening, when the two were alone, Mr. Bell remarked, 'If I could make a current of electricity vary in intensity precisely as the air varies in density during the production of sound, I should be able to transmit speech telegraphically.' This was his first allusion to the telephone but that the idea of such an instrument had been for some time in his mind was evident by the fact that he sketched in for Watson the kind of apparatus he thought necessary for such a device and they speculated concerning its construction. The project never went any farther, however, because Mr. Thomas Saunders and Mr. Gardiner Hubbard, who were financing Mr. Bell's experiments, felt the chances of this contrivance working satisfactorily were too uncertain. Already much time and money had been spent on the harmonic telegraph and they argued this scheme should be completed before a new venture was tried."

"I suppose that point of view was quite justifiable," mused Ted. "But wasn't it a pity?"

"Yes, it was," agreed Mr. Hazen. "Yet here again we realize how man moves inch by inch, never knowing what is just around the turn of the road. He can only go it blindly and do the best he knows at the time. Naturally neither Mr. Hubbard nor Mr. Saunders wanted to swamp any more money until they had received results for what they had spent already; and those results, alas, were not forthcoming. Over and over again poor Watson blamed himself lest some imperceptible defect in his part of the work was responsible for Mr. Bell's lack of success. The spring of 1875 came and still no light glimmered on the horizon. The harmonic telegraph seemed as far away from completion as ever. Patiently the men plodded on. Then on a June day, a day that began even less auspiciously than had other days, the heavens suddenly opened and Alexander Graham Bell had his vision!"

"What was it?"

"Tell us about it!" cried both boys in a breath.

"It was a warm, close afternoon in the loft over the Williams's shop and the transmitters and receivers were whining there more dolefully than usual. Several of them, sensitive to the weather, were out of tune, and as Mr. Bell had trained his ear to sounds until it was abnormally acute, he was tuning the springs of the receivers to the pitch of the transmitters, a service he always preferred to perform himself. To do this he placed the receiver against his ear and called to Watson, who was in the adjoining room, to start the current through the electromagnet of the corresponding transmitter. When this was done, Mr. Bell was able to turn a screw and adjust the instrument to the pitch desired. Watson admits in a book he has himself written that he was out of spirits that day and feeling irritable and impatient. The whiners had got on his nerves, I fancy. One of the springs that he was trying to start appeared to stick and in order to force it to vibrate he gave it a quick snap with his finger. Still it would not go and he snapped it sharply several times. Immediately there was a cry from Mr. Bell who rushed into the hall, exclaiming, 'What did you do then? Don't change anything. Let me see.'

"Watson was alarmed. Had he knocked out the entire circuit or what had he done in his fit of temper? Well, there was no escape from confession now; no pretending he had not vented his nervousness on the mechanism before him. With honesty he told the truth and even illustrated his hasty action. The thing was simple enough. In some way the make-and-break points of the transmitter spring had become welded together so that even when Watson snapped the instrument the circuit had remained unbroken, while by means of the piece of magnetized steel vibrating over the pole of the magnet an electric current was generated, the type of current that did exactly what Mr. Bell had dreamed of a current doing—a current of electricity that varied in intensity precisely as the air within the radius of that particular spring was varying in density. And not only did that undulatory current pass through the wire to the receiver Mr. Bell was holding, but as good luck would have it the mechanism was such that it transformed that current back into a faint but unmistakable echo of the sound issuing from the vibrating spring that generated it. But a fact more fortunate than all this was that the one man to whom the incident carried significance had the instrument at his ear at that particular moment. That was pure chance—a Heaven-sent, miraculous coincidence! But that Mr. Bell recognized the value and importance of that whispered echo that reached him over the wire and knew, when he heard it, that it was the embodiment of the idea that had been haunting him—that was not chance; it was genius!"

The room had been tensely still and now both boys drew a sigh of relief.

"How strange!" murmured Ted in an awed tone.

"Yes, it was like magic, was it not?" replied the tutor. "For the speaking telephone was born at that moment. Whatever practical work was necessary to make the invention perfect (and there were many, many details to be solved) was done afterward. But on June 2, 1875, the telephone as Bell had dreamed it came into the world. That single demonstration on that hot morning in Williams's shop proved myriad facts to the inventor. One was that if a mechanism could transmit the many complex vibrations of one sound it could do the same for any sound, even human speech. He saw now that the intricate paraphernalia he had supposed necessary to achieve his long-imagined result was not to be needed, for did not the simple contrivance in his hand do the trick? The two men in the stuffy little loft could scarcely contain their delight. For hours they went on repeating the experiment in order to make sure they were really awake. They verified their discovery beyond all shadow of doubt. One spring and then another was tried and always the same great law acted with invariable precision. Heat, fatigue, even the dingy garret itself was forgotten in the flight of those busy, exultant hours. Before they separated that night, Alexander Graham Bell had given to Thomas Watson directions for making the first electric speaking telephone in the world!"

CHAPTER X

WHAT CAME AFTERWARD

"Was that first telephone like ours?" inquired Ted later as, their lunch finished, they sat idly looking out at the river.

"Not wholly. Time has improved the first crude instrument," Mr. Hazen replied. "The initial principle of the telephone, however, has never varied from Mr. Bell's primary idea. Before young Watson tumbled into bed on that epoch-making night, he had finished the instrument Bell had asked him to have ready, every part of it being made by the eager assistant who probably only faintly realized the mammoth importance of his task. Yet whether he realized it or not, he had caught a sufficient degree of the inventor's excitement to urge him forward. Over one of the receivers, as Mr. Bell directed, he mounted a small drumhead of goldbeater's skin, joined the center of it to the free end of the receiver spring, and arranged a mouthpiece to talk into. The plan was to force the steel spring to answer the vibrations of the voice and at the same time generate a current of electricity that should vary in intensity just as the air varies in density during the utterance of speech sounds. Not only did Watson make this instrument as specified, but in his interest he went even farther, and as the rooms in the loft seemed too near together, the tireless young man ran a special wire from the attic down the two flights of stairs to the ground floor of the shop and ended it near his workbench at the rear of the building, thus constructing the first telephone line in history.

"Then the next day Mr. Bell came to test out his invention and, as you can imagine, there was great excitement."

"I hope it worked," put in Laurie.

"It worked all right although at this early stage of the game it was hardly to be expected that the instrument produced was perfect. Nevertheless, the demonstration proved that the principle behind it was sound and that was all Mr. Bell really wanted to make sure of. Watson, as it chanced, got far more out of this initial performance than did Mr. Bell himself for because of the inventor's practical work in phonics the vibrations of his voice carried more successfully than did those of the assistant. Yet the youthful Watson was not without his compensations. Nature had blessed him with unusually acute hearing and as a result he could catch Bell's tones perfectly as they came over the wire and could almost distinguish his words; but shout as he would, poor Mr. Bell could not hear *him*. This dilemma nevertheless discouraged neither of them for Watson had plenty of energy and was quite willing to leap up the two flights of stairs and repeat what he had heard; and this report greatly reassured Mr. Bell, who outlined a list of other improvements for another telephone that should be ready on the following day."

"I suppose they kept remodelling the telephones all the time after that, didn't they?" inquired Ted.

"You may be sure they did," was Mr. Hazen's response. "The harmonic telegraph was entirely sidetracked and the interest of both men turned into this newer channel. Mr. Bell, in the meantime, was giving less and less energy to his teaching and more and more to his inventing. Before many days the two could talk back and forth and hear one another's voices without difficulty, although ten full months of hard work was necessary before they were able to understand what was said. It was not until after this long stretch of patient toil that Watson unmistakably heard Mr. Bell say one day, '*Mr. Watson, please come here, I want you.*' The message was a very ordinary, untheatrical one for a moment so significant, but neither of the enthusiasts heeded that. The thrilling fact was that the words had come clear-cut over the wire."

"Gee!" broke in Laurie.

"It certainly must have been a dramatic moment," Mr. Hazen agreed. "Mr. Bell, now convinced beyond all doubt of the value of his idea, hired two rooms at a cheap boarding-house situated at Number 5 Exeter Place, Boston. In one of these he slept and in the other he equipped a laboratory. Watson connected these rooms by a wire and afterward all Mr. Bell's experimenting was done here instead of at the Williams's shop. It was at the Exeter Place rooms that this first wonderful message came to Watson's ears. From this period on the telephone took rapid strides forward. By the summer of 1876, it had been improved until a simple sentence was understandable if carefully repeated three or four times."

"Repeated three or four times!" gasped Laurie in dismay.

The tutor smiled at the boy's incredulousness.

"You forget we are not dealing with a finished product," said he gently. "I am a little afraid you would have been less patient with the imperfections of an infant invention than were Bell and Watson."

"I know I should," was the honest retort.

"The telephone was a very delicate instrument to perfect,"

explained Mr. Hazen. "Always remember that. An inventor must not only be a man who has unshaken faith in his idea but he must also have the courage to cling stubbornly to his belief through every sort of mechanical vicissitude. This Mr. Bell did. June of 1876 was the year of the great Centennial at Philadelphia, the year that marked the first century of our country's progress. As the exhibition was to be one symbolic of our national development in every line, Mr. Bell decided to show his telephone there; to this end he set Watson, who was still at the Williams's shop, to making exhibition telephones of the two varieties they had thus far worked out."

"I'll bet Watson was almighty proud of his job," Ted interrupted.

"I fancy he was and certainly he had a right to be," answered Mr. Hazen. "I have always been glad, too, that it fell to his lot to have this honor; for he had worked long and faithfully, and if there were glory to be had, he should share it. To his unflagging zeal and intelligence Mr. Bell owed a great deal. Few men could so whole-heartedly have effaced their own personality and thrown themselves with such zest into the success of another as did Thomas Watson."

The tutor paused.

"Up to this time," he presently went on, "the telephones used by Bell and Watson in their experiments had been very crude affairs; but those designed for the Centennial were glorified objects. Watson says that you could see your face in them. The Williams's shop outdid itself and more splendid instruments never went forth from its doors. You can therefore imagine Watson's chagrin when, after highly commending Mr. Bell's invention, Sir William Thompson added, '*This, perhaps, greatest marvel hitherto achieved by electric telegraph has been obtained by appliances of quite a homespun and rudimentary character.*'"

Both Ted and Laurie joined in the laughter of the tutor.

"And now the telephone was actually launched?" Ted asked.

"Well, it was not really in clear waters," Mr. Hazen replied, with a dubious shrug of his shoulders, "but at least there was no further question as to which of his schemes Mr. Bell should perfect. Both Mr. Hubbard and Mr. Saunders, who were assisting him financially, agreed that for the present it must be the telephone; and recognizing the value of Watson's services, they offered him an interest in Mr. Bell's patents if he would give up his work at Williams's shop and put in all his time on this device. Nevertheless they did not entirely abandon the harmonic telegraph for Bell's success with the other invention had only served to strengthen their confidence in his ability and genius. It was also decided that Mr. Bell should move from Salem to Boston, take an additional room at the Exeter Place house (which would give him the entire floor where his laboratory was), and unhampered by further teaching plunge into the inventive career for which heaven had so richly endowed him and which he loved with all his heart. You can picture to yourselves the joy these decisions gave him and the eagerness with which he and Watson took up their labors together.

"They made telephones of every imaginable size in their attempts to find out whether there was anything that would work more satisfactorily than the type they now had. But in spite of their many experiments they came back to the kind of instrument with which they had started, discovering nothing that was superior to their original plan. Except that they compelled the transmitter to do double duty and act also as a receiver, the telephone that emerged from these many tests was practically similar in principle to the one of to-day."

"Had they made any long-distance trials up to this time?" questioned Laurie.

"No," Mr. Hazen admitted. "They had lacked opportunity to make such tests since no great span of wires was accessible to them. But on October 9, 1876, the Walworth Manufacturing Company gave them permission to try out their device on the Company's private telegraph line that ran from Boston to Cambridge. The distance to be sure was only two miles but it might as well have been two thousand so far as the excitement of the two workers went. Their baby had never been out of doors. Now at last it was to take the air! Fancy how thrilling the prospect was! As the wire over which they were to make the experiment was in use during the day, they were forced to wait until the plant was closed for the night. Then Watson, with his tools and his telephone under his arm, went to the Cambridge office where he impatiently listened for Mr. Bell's signal to come over the Morse sounder. When he had heard this and thereby made certain that Bell was at the other end of the line, he cut out the sounder, connected the telephone he had brought with him, and put his ear to the transmitter."

The hut was so still one could almost hear the breathing of the lads, who were listening intently.

"Go on!" Laurie said quickly. "Tell us what happened."

"*Nothing happened!*" answered the tutor. "Watson listened but there was not a sound."

"Great Scott!"

"The poor assistant was aghast," went on Mr. Hazen. "He was at a complete loss to understand what was the matter. Could it be that the contrivance which worked so promisingly in the Boston rooms would not work under these other conditions? Perhaps an electric current was too delicate a thing to carry sound very far. Or was it that the force of the vibration filtered off at each insulator along the line until it became too feeble to be heard? All these possibilities flashed into Watson's mind while at his post two miles away from Mr. Bell he struggled to readjust the instrument. Then suddenly an inspiration came to his alert brain. Might there not be another Morse sounder somewhere about? If there were, that would account for the whole difficulty. Springing up, he began to search the room and after following the wires, sure enough, he traced them to a relay with a high resistance coil in the circuit. Feverishly he cut this out and rushed back to his telephone. Plainly over the wire came Bell's voice, '*Ahoy! Ahoy!* For a few seconds both of them were too delighted to say much of anything else. Then they sobered down and began this first long-distance conversation. Now one of the objections Mr. Bell had constantly been forced to meet from the skeptical public was that while the telegraph delivered messages that were of unchallenged accuracy, telephone conversations were liable to errors of misunderstanding. One could not therefore rely so completely on the trustworthiness of the latter as on that of the former. To refute this charge Mr. Bell had insisted that both he and Watson carefully write out whatever they heard that the two records might afterward be compared and verified. '*That is,*' Mr. Bell had added with the flicker of a smile, '*if we succeed in talking at all!*' Well, they did succeed, as you have heard. At first they held only a stilted dialogue and conscientiously jotted it down; but afterward their exuberance got the better of them and in sheer joy they chattered away like magpies until long past midnight. Then, loath to destroy the connection, Watson detached his telephone, replaced the Company's wires, and set out for Boston. In the meantime Mr. Bell, who had previously made an arrangement with the *Boston Advertiser* to publish on the following morning an account of the experiment, together with the recorded conversations, had gone to the newspaper office to carry his material to the press. Hence he was not at the Exeter Place rooms when the jubilant Watson arrived. But the early morning hour did not daunt the young electrician; and when, after some delay, Mr. Bell came in, the two men rushed toward one another and regardless of everything else executed what Mr. Watson has since characterized as a *war dance.* Certainly they were quite justified in their rejoicings and perhaps if their landlady had understood the cause of their exultations she might have joined in the dance herself. Unluckily she had only a scant sympathy with inventive genius and since the victory celebration not only aroused her, but also wakened most of her boarders from their slumbers, her ire was great and the next morning she informed the two men that if they could not be more quiet at night they would have to leave her house."

An appreciative chuckle came from the listeners.

"If she had known what she was sheltering, I suppose she would have been proud as a peacock and promptly told all her neighbors," grinned Ted.

"Undoubtedly! But she did not know, poor soul!" returned Mr. Hazen.

"After this Mr. Bell and Mr. Watson must have shot ahead by leaps and bounds," commented Laurie.

"There is no denying that that two-mile test did give them both courage and assurance," responded the tutor. "They got chances to try out the invention on longer telegraph wires; and in spite of the fact that no such thing as hard-drawn copper wire was in existence they managed to get results even over rusty wires with their unsoldered joinings. Through such experiments an increasingly wider circle of outside persons heard of the telephone and the marvel began to attract greater attention. Mr. Bell's modest little laboratory became the mecca of scientists and visitors of every imaginable type. Moses G. Farmer, well known in the electrical world, came to view the wonder and confessed to Mr. Bell that more than once he had lingered on the threshold of the same mighty discovery but had never been able to step across it into success. It amused both Mr. Bell and Mr. Watson to see how embarrassed persons were when allowed to talk over the wire. Standing up and speaking into a box has long since become too much a matter of course with us to appear ridiculous; but those experiencing the novelty for the first time were so overwhelmed by self-consciousness that they could think of nothing to say. One day when Mr. Watson called from his end of the line, 'How do you do?' a dignified lawyer who was trying the instrument answered with a foolish giggle, 'Rig-a-jig-jig and away we go!' The psychological reaction was too much for many a well-poised individual and I do not wonder it was, do you?"

"It must have been almost as good as a vaudeville show to watch the people," commented Ted.

"Better! Lots better!" echoed Laurie.

"In April, 1877, the first out-of-door telephone line running on its own private wires was installed in the shop of Charles Williams at Number 109 Court Street and carried from there out to his house at Somerville. Quite a little ceremony marked the event. Both Mr. Bell and Mr. Watson attended the christening and the papers chronicled the circumstance in bold headlines the following day. Immediately patrons who wanted telephones began to pop up right and left like so many mushrooms. But alas, where was the money to come from that should enable Mr. Bell and his associates to branch out and grasp the opportunities that now beckoned them? The inventor's own resources were at a low ebb; Watson, like many another young man, had more brains than fortune; and neither Mr. Hubbard nor Mr. Saunders felt they could provide the necessary capital. Already the Western Union had refused Mr. Hubbard's offer to sell all Mr. Bell's patents for one hundred thousand dollars, the Company feeling that the price asked was much too high. Two years later, however, they would willingly have paid twenty-five million dollars for the privilege they had so summarily scorned. What was to be done? Money must be secured for without it all further progress was at a standstill. Was success to be sacrificed now that the goal was well within sight? And must the telephone be shut away from the public and never take its place of service in the great world? Why, if a thing was not to be used it might almost as well never have been invented! The spirits of the telephone pioneers sank lower and lower. The only way to raise money seemed to be to sell the telephone instruments outright and this Mr. Bell, who desired simply to lease them, was unwilling to do. Then an avenue of escape from this dilemma presented itself to him."

"What was it?" asked Laurie.

"He would give lectures, accompanying them with practical demonstrations of the telephone. This would bring in money and banish for a time, at least, the possibility of having to sell instead of rent telephones. The plan succeeded admirably. The first lecture was given at Salem where, because of Mr. Bell's previous residence and many friends, a large audience packed the hall. Then Boston desired to know more of the invention and an appeal for a lecture signed by Longfellow, Oliver Wendell Holmes, and other distinguished citizens was forwarded to Mr. Bell. The Boston lectures were followed by others in New York, Providence, and the principal cities throughout New England."

"It seems a shame Mr. Bell should have had to take his time to do that, doesn't it?" mused Ted. "How did they manage the lectures?"

"The lectures had a checkered existence," smiled Mr. Hazen. "Many very amusing incidents centered about them. Were I to talk until doomsday I could not begin to tell you the multitudinous adventures Mr. Bell and Mr. Watson had during their platform career; for although Mr. Watson was never really before the footlights as Mr. Bell was, he was an indispensable part of the show,—the power behind the scenes, the man at the other end of the wire, who furnished the lecture hall with such stunts as would not only convince an audience but also entertain them. It was a dull, thankless position, perhaps, to be so far removed from the excitement and glamor, to be always playing or singing into a little wooden box and never catching a glimpse of the fun that was going on at the other end of the line; but since Mr. Watson was a rather shy person it is possible he was quite as well pleased. After all, it was Mr. Bell whom everybody wanted to see and of course Mr. Watson understood this. Therefore he was quite content to act his modest rôle and not only gather together at his end of the wire cornet soloists, electric organs, brass bands, or whatever startling novelties the occasion demanded, but talk or sing himself. The shyest of men can sometimes out-Herod Herod if not obliged to face their listeners in person. As Watson had spoken so much over the telephone, he was thoroughly accustomed to it and played the parts assigned him far better than more gifted but less practically trained soloists did. It always amused him intensely after he had bellowed *Pull for the Shore, Hold the Fort* or *Yankee Doodle* into the transmitter to hear the applause that followed his efforts. Probably singing before a large company was about the last thing Tom Watson expected his electrical career would lead him into. Had he been told that such a fate awaited him, he would doubtless have jeered at the prophecy. But here he was, singing away with all his lung power, before a great hall full of people and not minding it in the least; nay, I rather think he may have enjoyed it. Once, desiring to give a finer touch than usual to the entertainment, Mr. Bell hired a professional singer; but this soloist had never used a telephone and although he possessed the art of singing he was not able to get it across the wire. No one in the lecture hall could hear him. Mr. Bell promptly summoned Watson (who was doubtless congratulating himself on being off duty) to render *Hold the Fort* in his customary lusty fashion. After this Mr. Watson became the star soloist and no more singers were engaged."

A ripple of amusement passed over the faces of the lads listening.

"Ironically enough, as Mr. Watson's work kept him always in the background furnishing the features of these entertainments, he never himself heard Mr. Bell lecture. He says, however, that the great inventor was a very polished, magnetic speaker who never failed to secure and hold the attention of his hearers. Of course, every venture has its trials and these lecture tours were no exception to the general rule. Once, for example, the Northern Lights were responsible for demoralizing the current and spoiling a telephone demonstration at Lawrence; and although both Watson and a cornetist strained their lungs to bursting, neither of them could be heard at the hall. Then the sparks began to play over the wires and the show had to be called off. Nevertheless such disasters occurred seldom, and for the most part the performances went smoothly, the people were delighted, and Mr. Bell increased not only his fame but his fortune."

Mr. Hazen stopped a moment.

"You must not for an instant suppose," he resumed presently, "that the telephone was a perfected product. Transmitters of sufficient delicacy to do away with shouting and screaming had not yet made their appearance and in consequence when one telephoned all the world knew it; it was not until the Blake transmitter came into use that a telephone conversation could be to any extent confidential. In its present state, the longer the range the more lung power was demanded; and probably had not this been the condition, people would have shouted anyway, simply from instinct. Even with our own delicately adjusted instruments we are prone to forget and commit this folly. But in the early days one was forced to uplift his voice at the telephone and if he had no voice to uplift woe betide his telephoning. And apropos of this matter, I recall reading that once, when Mr. Bell was to lecture in New York, he thought what a drawing card it would be if he could have his music and other features of entertainment come from Boston. Therefore he arranged to use the wires of the Atlantic and Pacific Telegraph Company and to this end he and Watson planned a dress rehearsal at midnight in order to try out the inspiration. Now it chanced that the same inflexible landlady ruled at Number 5 Exeter Place, and remembering his former experience, Mr. Watson felt something must be done to stifle the shouting he foresaw he would be compelled to do at that nocturnal hour. So he gathered together all the blankets and rolled them into a sort of cone and to the small end of this he tied his telephone. Then he crept into this stuffy, breathless shelter, the ancestor of our sound-proof telephone booth, and for nearly three hours shouted to Mr. Bell in New York—or tried to. But the experiment was not a success. He could be heard, it is true, but not distinctly enough to risk such an unsatisfactory demonstration before an uninitiated audience. Hence the scheme was abandoned and Mr. Watson scrambled his things together and betook himself to a point nearer the center of action."

"It must all have been great fun, mustn't it?" said Laurie thoughtfully.

"Great fun, no doubt, but very hard work," was the tutor's answer. "Many a long, discouraging hour was yet to follow before the telephone became a factor in the everyday world. Yet each step of the climb to success had its sunlight as well as its shadow, its humor as well as its pathos; and it was fortunate both men appreciated this fact for it floated them over many a rough sea. Man can spare almost any other attribute better than his sense of humor. Without this touchstone he is ill equipped to battle with life," concluded Mr. Hazen whimsically.

CHAPTER XI

THE REST OF THE STORY

"I should think," commented Laurie one day, when Ted and Mr. Hazen were sitting in his room, "that Mr. Bell's landlady would have fussed no end to have his telephone ringing all the time."

"My dear boy, you do not for an instant suppose that the telephones of that period had bells, do you?" replied Mr. Hazen with amusement. "No, indeed! There was no method for signaling. Unless two persons agreed to talk at a specified hour of the day or night and timed their conversation by the clock, or else had recourse to the Morse code, there was no satisfactory way they could call one another. This did not greatly matter when you recollect how few telephones there were in existence. Mr. Williams used to summon a listener by tapping on the metal diaphragm of the instrument with his pencil, a practice none too beneficial to the transmitter; nor was the resulting sound powerful enough to reach any one who was not close at hand. Furthermore, persons could not stand and hold their telephones and wait until they could arouse the party at the other end of the line for a telephone weighed almost ten pounds and——"

"Ten pounds!" repeated Ted in consternation.

Mr. Hazen nodded.

"Yes," answered he, "the early telephones were heavy, cumbersome objects and not at all like the trim, compact instruments we have to-day. In fact, they were quite similar to the top of a sewing-machine box, only, perhaps, they were a trifle smaller. You can understand that one would not care to carry on a very long conversation if he must in the meantime stand and hold in his arms a ten-pound object about ten inches long, six inches wide, and six inches high."

"I should say not!" Laurie returned. "It must have acted as a fine check, though, on people who just wanted to gabble."

Both Ted and the tutor laughed.

"Of course telephone owners could not go on that way," Ted said, after the merriment had subsided. "What did Mr. Bell do about it?"

"The initial step for betterment was not taken by Mr. Bell but by Mr. Watson," Mr. Hazen responded. "He rigged a little hammer inside the box and afterwards put a button on the outside. This *thumper* was the first calling device ever in use. Later on, however, the assistant felt he could improve on this method and he adapted the buzzer of the harmonic telegraph to the telephone; this proved to be a distinct advance over the more primitive *thumper* but nevertheless he was not satisfied with it as a signaling apparatus. So he searched farther still, and with the aid of one of the shabby little books on electricity that he had purchased for a quarter from Williams's tiny showcase, he evolved the magneto-electric call bell such as we use to-day. This answered every purpose and nothing has ever been found that has supplanted it. It is something of a pity that Watson did not think to affix his name to this invention; but he was too deeply interested in what he was doing and probably too busy to consider its value. His one idea was to help Mr. Bell to improve the telephone in every way possible and measuring what he was going to get out of it was apparently very far from his thought. Of course, the first of these call bells were not perfect, any more than were the first telephones; by and by, however, their defects were remedied until they became entirely satisfactory."

"So they now had telephones, transmitters, and call bells," reflected Ted. "I should say they were pretty well ready for business."

"You forget the switchboard," was Mr. Hazen's retort. "A one-party line was a luxury and a thing practically beyond the reach of the public. At best there were very few of them. No, some method for connecting parties who wished to speak to one another had to be found and it is at this juncture of the telephone's career that a new contributor to the invention's success comes upon the scene.

"Doing business at Number 342 Washington Street was a young New Yorker by the name of Edwin T. Holmes, who had charge of his father's burglar-alarm office. As all the electrical equipment he used was made at Williams's shop, he used frequently to go there and one day, when he entered, he came upon Charles Williams, the proprietor of the store, standing before a little box that rested on a shelf and shouting into it. Hearing Mr. Holmes's step, he glanced over his shoulder, met his visitor's astonished gaze, and laughed.

"'For Heaven's sake, Williams, what have you got in that box?' demanded Mr. Holmes.

"'Oh, this is what that fellow out there by Watson's bench, Mr. Bell, calls a telephone,' replied Mr. Williams.

"'So that's the thing I have seen squibs in the paper about!' observed the burglar-alarm man with curiosity.

"'Yes, he and Watson have been working at it for some time.'

"Now Mr. Holmes knew Tom Watson well for the young

electrician had done a great deal of work for him in the past; moreover, the New York man was a person who kept well abreast of the times and was always alert for novel ideas. Therefore quite naturally he became interested in the embryo enterprise and dropped into Williams's shop almost every day to see how the infant invention was progressing. In this way he met both Mr. Gardiner Hubbard and Mr. Thomas Saunders, who were Mr. Bell's financial sponsors. After Mr. Holmes had been a spectator of the telephone for some time, he remarked to Mr. Hubbard:

"'If you succeed in getting two or three of those things to work and will lend them to me, I will show them to Boston.'

"'Show them to Boston,' repeated Mr. Hubbard. 'How will you do that?'

"'Well,' said Mr. Holmes, 'I have a Central Office down at Number 342 Washington Street from which I have individual wires running to most of the banks, many jeweler's shops, and other stores. I can ring a bell in a bank from my office and the bank can ring one to me in return. By using switches and giving a prearranged signal to the Exchange Bank, both of us could throw a switch which would put the telephones in circuit and we could talk together.'

"After looking at Mr. Holmes for a moment with great surprise, Mr. Hubbard slapped him on the back and said, 'I will do it! Get your switches and other things ready.'

"Of course Mr. Holmes was greatly elated to be the first one to show on his wires this wonderful new instrument and connect two or more parties through a Central Office. He immediately had a switchboard made (its actual size was five by thirty-six inches) through which he ran a few of his burglar-alarm circuits and by means of plugs he arranged so that he could throw the circuit from the burglar-alarm instruments to the telephone.

He also had a shelf made to rest the telephones on and had others like it built at the Exchange National and the Hide and Leather banks. In a few days the telephones, numbered 6, 7, and 8, arrived and were quickly installed, and the marvellous exhibition opened. Soon two more instruments were added, one of which was placed in the banking house of Brewster, Bassett and Company and the other in the Shoe and Leather Bank. When the Williams shop was connected, it gave Mr. Holmes a working exchange of five connections, the first telephone exchange in history."

"I'll bet they had some queer times with it," asserted Ted.

"They did, indeed!" smiled Mr. Hazen. "The papers announced the event, although in very retiring type, and persons of every walk in life flocked to the Holmes office to see the wonder with their own eyes. So many came that Mr. Holmes had a long bench made so that visitors could sit down and watch the show. One day a cornetist played from the Holmes building so that the members of the Boston Stock Exchange, assembled at the office of Brewster, Bassett and Company, could hear the performance. Considering the innovation a great boon, the New York man secured another instrument and after meditating some time on whom he would bestow it he decided to install it in the Revere Bank, thinking the bank people would be delighted to be recipients of the favor. His burglar-alarm department had pass-keys to all the banks and therefore, when banking hours were over, he and one of his men obtained entrance and put the telephone in place. The following morning he had word that the president of the bank wished to see him and expecting to receive thanks for the happy little surprise he had given the official, he hurried to the bank. Instead of expressing gratitude, however, the president of the institution said in an injured tone:

"'Mr. Holmes, what is that play toy you have taken the liberty of putting up out there in the banking room?'

"'Why, that is what they are going to call a telephone,' explained Mr. Holmes.

"'A telephone! What's a telephone?' inquired the president.

"With enthusiasm the New Yorker carefully sketched in the new invention and told what could be done with it.

"After he had finished he was greatly astonished to have the head of the bank reply with scorn:

"'Mr. Holmes, you take that plaything out of my bank and don't ever take such liberties again.'

"You may be sure the *plaything* was quickly removed and the Revere Bank went on record as having the first telephone disconnection in the country.

"Having exhibited the telephones for a couple of weeks, Mr. Holmes went to Mr. Hubbard and suggested that he would like to continue to carry on the exchange but he should like it put on a business basis.

"'Have you any money?' asked Mr. Hubbard.

"'Mighty little,' was the frank answer.

"'Well, that's more than we have got,' Mr. Hubbard responded. 'However, if you have got enough money to do the business and build the exchange, we will rent you the telephones.'

"By August, 1877, when Bell's patent was sixteen months' old, Casson's History tells us there were seven hundred and seventy-eight telephones in use and the Bell Telephone Association was formed. The organization was held together by an extremely simple agreement which gave Bell, Hubbard, and Saunders a three-tenths' interest apiece in the patents and Watson one-tenth. The business possessed no capital, as there was none to be had; and these four men at that time had an absolute monopoly of the telephone business,—and everybody else was quite willing they should have.

"In addition to these four associates was Charles Williams, who had from the first been a believer in the venture, and Mr. Holmes who built the first telephone exchange with his own money, and had about seven hundred of the seven hundred and seventy-eight instruments on his wires. Mr. Robert W. Devonshire joined the others in August, 1877, as bookkeeper and general secretary and has since become an official in the American Telephone and Telegraph Company.

"Mr. Holmes rented the telephones for ten dollars a year and through his exchange was the first practical man who had the temerity to offer telephone service for sale. It was the arrival of a new idea in the business world.

"Now the business world is not a tranquil place and as soon as the new invention began to prosper, every sort of difficulty beset its path.

"There were those who denied that Mr. Bell had been first in the field with the telephone idea, and they began to contest his right to the patents. Other telephone companies sprang up and began to compete with the rugged-hearted pioneers who had launched the industry. Lawsuits followed and for years Mr. Bell's days were one continual fight to maintain his claims and keep others from wresting his hard-earned prosperity from him. But in time smoother waters were reached and now Alexander Graham Bell has been universally conceded to be the inventor of this marvel without which we of the present should scarcely know how to get on."

"I don't believe we could live without telephones now, do you?" remarked Laurie thoughtfully.

"Oh, I suppose we could keep alive," laughed Mr. Hazen,

"but I am afraid our present order of civilization would have to be changed a good deal. We scarcely realize what a part the telephone plays in almost everything we attempt to do. Certainly the invention helps to speed up our existence; and, convenient as it is, I sometimes am ungrateful enough to wonder whether we should not be a less highly strung and nervous nation without it. However that may be, the telephone is here, and here to stay, and you now have a pretty clear idea of its early history. How from these slender beginnings the industry spread until it spanned continents and circled the globe, you can easily read elsewhere. Yet mighty as this factor has become in the business world, it is not from this angle of its greatness that I like best to view it. I would rather think of the lives it has saved; the good news it has often borne; the misunderstandings it has prevented; the better unity it has promoted among all peoples. Just as the railroad was a gigantic agent in bringing North, South, East, and West closer together, so the telephone has helped to make our vast country, with its many diverse elements, 'one nation, indivisible.'"

CHAPTER XII

CONSPIRATORS

With September a tint of scarlet crept into the foliage bordering the little creeks that stole from the river into the Aldercliffe meadows; tangles of goldenrod and purple asters breathed of autumn, and the mornings were now too chilly for a swim. Had it not been for the great fireplace the shack would not have been livable. For the first time both Ted and Laurie realized that the summer they had each enjoyed so heartily was at an end and they were face to face with a different phase of life.

The harvest, with its horde of vegetables and fruit, had been gathered into the yawning barns and cellars and the earth that had given so patiently of its increase had earned the right to lay fallow until the planting of another spring. Ted's work was done. He had helped deposit the last barrel of ruddy apples, the last golden pumpkins within doors, and now he had nothing more to do but to pack up his possessions preparatory to returning to Freeman's Falls, there to rejoin his family and continue his studies.

Once the thought that the drudgery of summer was over would have been a delightful one. Why, he could remember the exultation with which he had burned the last cornstalks at the end of the season when at home in Vermont. The ceremony had been a rite of hilarious rejoicing. But this year, strange to say, a dull sadness stole over him whenever he looked upon the devastated gardens and the reaches of bare brown earth. There was nothing to keep him longer either at Aldercliffe or Pine Lea. His work henceforth lay at school.

It was strange that a little sigh accompanied the thought for had he not always looked forward to this very prospect? What was the matter now? Was not studying the thing he had longed to be free to do? Why this regret and depression? And why was his own vague sadness reflected in Laurie's eyes and in those of Mr. Hazen? Summer could not last forever; it was childish to ask that it should. They all had known from the beginning that these days of companionship must slip away and come to an end. And yet the end had come so quickly. Why, it had scarcely been midsummer before the twilight had deepened and the days mellowed into autumn.

Well, they had held many happy, happy hours for Ted, at least. Never had he dreamed of such pleasures. He had enjoyed his work, constant though it had been, and had come to cherish as much pride in the gardens of Aldercliffe and Pine Lea, in the vast crops of hay that bulged from the barn lofts, as if they had been his own. And when working hours were over there was Laurie Fernald and the new and pleasant friendship that existed between them.

As Ted began to drag out from beneath his bunk the empty wooden boxes he purposed to pack his books in, his heart sank. Soon the cosy house in which he had passed so many perfect hours would be quite denuded. Frosts would nip the flowers nodding in a final glory of color outside the windows; the telephone would be disconnected; his belongings would once more be crowded into the stuffy little flat at home; and the door of the camp on the river's edge would be tightly locked on a deserted paradise.

Of course, everything had to come to an end some time and often when he had been weeding long, and what seemed interminable rows of seedlings and had been making only feeble progress at the task, the thought that termination of his task was an ultimate certainty had been a consolation mighty and sustaining. Such an uninteresting undertaking could not last forever, he told himself over and over again; nothing ever did. And now with ironic conformity to law, his philosophy had turned on him, demonstrating beyond cavil that not only did the things one longed to be free of come to a sure finality but so did those one pined to have linger.

Although night was approaching, too intent had he been on his reveries to notice that the room was in darkness. How still everything was! That was the way the little hut would be after he was gone,—cold, dark, and silent. He wondered as he sat there whether he should ever come back. Would the Fernalds want him next season and again offer him the boathouse for a home? They had said nothing about it but if he thought he was to return another summer it would not be so hard to go now. It was leaving forever that saddened him.

He must have remained immovable there in the twilight for a much longer time than he realized; and perhaps he would have sat there even longer had not a sound startled him into breathless attention. It was the rhythmic stroke of a canoe paddle and as it came nearer it was intermingled with the whispers of muffled voices. Possibly he might have thought nothing of the happening had there not been a note of tense caution in the words that came to his ear.

Who could be navigating the river at this hour of the night?

Surely not pleasure-seekers, for it was very cold and an approaching storm had clouded in the sky until it had become a dome of velvet blackness. Whoever was venturing out upon the river must either know the stream very well or be reckless of his own safety.

Ted did not move but listened intently.

"Let's take a chance and land," he heard a thick voice murmur. "The boy has evidently either gone to bed or he isn't here. Whichever the case, he can do us no harm and I'm not for risking the river any farther. It's black as midnight. We might get into the current and have trouble."

"What's the sense of running our heads into a noose by landing?" objected a second speaker. "We can't talk here—that's nonsense."

"I tell you the boy isn't in the hut," retorted his comrade. "I remember now that I heard he was going back to the Falls to school. Likely he has gone already. In any case we can try the door and examine the windows; if the place is locked, we shall be sure he is not here. And should it prove to be inhabited, we can easy hatch up some excuse for coming. He'll be none the wiser. Even if he should be here," added the man after a pause, "he is probably asleep. After a hard day's work a boy his age sleeps like a log. There'll be no waking him, so don't fret. Come! Let's steer for the float."

"But I——"

"Great Heavens, Cronin! We've got to take some chances. You're not getting cold feet so soon, are you?" burst out the other scornfully.

"N—o! Of course not," his companion declared with forced bravado. "But I don't like taking needless risks. The boy might be awake and hear us."

"What if he does? Haven't I told you I will invent some yarn to put him off the scent? He wouldn't be suspecting mischief, anyhow. I tell you I'm not going drifting round this river in the dark any longer. Next thing we know we may hit a snag and upset."

"But you insisted on coming."

"I know I did," snapped the sharp voice. "What chance had we to talk in a crowded boarding-house whose very walls had ears? Or on the village streets? I knew the river would have no listeners and you see I was right; it hasn't. But I did expect there would be a trifle more light. It is like ink, isn't it? You can't see your hand before your face."

"I don't believe we could find the float even if we tried for it," piped his friend with malicious satisfaction.

"Find it? Of course we can. I've traveled this river too many times to get lost on it. I know every inch of the stream."

"But aren't there boats at the landing?"

"Oh, they've been hauled in for the season long ago. I know that to be a fact."

"Then I guess young Turner must have gone."

"That's what I've been trying to tell you for the last half-hour," asserted the other voice with high-pitched irritation. "Why waste all this time? Let's land, talk things over, lay our plans, and be getting back to Freeman's Falls. We mustn't be seen returning to the town together too late for it might arouse suspicion."

"You're right there."

"Then go ahead and paddle for the landing. I'll steer. Just have your hand out so we won't bump."

The lapping of the paddles came nearer and nearer. Then there was a crash as the nose of the canoe struck the float.

"You darned idiot, Cronin! Why didn't you fend her off as I told you to?"

"I couldn't see. I——"

"Hush!"

A moment of breathless silence followed and then there was a derisive laugh.

"I told you the boy wasn't here," one of the men declared aloud. "If he had been he would have had his head out the window by now. We've made noise enough to wake the dead."

"But he may be here for all that," cautioned the other speaker. "Don't talk so loud."

"Nonsense!" his comrade retorted without lowering his tone. "I tell you the boy has gone back home and the hut is as empty as a last year's bird's nest. I'll stake my oath on it. The place is shut and locked tight as a drum. You'll see I'm right presently."

Instantly Ted's brain was alert. The door was locked, that he knew, for when he came in he had bolted it for the night. One window, however, was open and he dared not attempt to close it lest he make some betraying sound; and even were he able to shut it noiselessly he reflected that the procedure would be an unwise one since it would cut him off from hearing the conversation. No, he must keep perfectly still and trust that his nocturnal visitors would not make too thorough an investigation of the premises.

To judge from the scuffling of feet outside, both of them had now alighted from the canoe and were approaching the door. Soon he heard a hand fumbling with the latch and afterward came a heavy knock.

Slipping breathlessly from his chair he crouched upon the floor, great beads of perspiration starting out on his forehead.

"The door is locked, as I told you," he heard some one mutter.

"He may be asleep."

"We can soon make sure. Ah, there! Turner! Turner!"

Once more a series of blows descended upon the wooden panel.

"Does that convince you, Cronin?"

"Y—e—s," owned Cronin reluctantly. "I guess he's gone."

"Of course he's gone! Come, brace up, can't you?" urged his companion. "Where's your backbone?"

"I'm not afraid."

"Tell that to the marines! You're timid and jumpy as a girl. How are we ever to put this thing over if you don't pull yourself together? I might as well have a baby to help me," sneered the gruff voice.

"Don't be so hard on me, Alf," whined his comrade. "I ain't done nothin'. Ain't I right here and ready?"

"You're here, all right," snarled the first speaker, "but whether you're ready or not is another matter. Now I'm going to give you a last chance to pull out. Do you want to go ahead or don't you? It's no good for us to be laying plans if you are going to be weak-kneed at the end and balk at carrying them out. Do you mean to stand by me and see this thing to a finish or don't you?"

"I—sure I do!"

"Cross your heart?"

"Cross my heart!" This time the words echoed with more positiveness.

"You're not going to back out or squeal?" his pal persisted.

"Why, Alf, how can you——"

"Because I've got to be sure before I stir another inch."

"But ain't I told you over and over again that I——"

"I don't trust you."

"What makes you so hard on a feller, Alf?" whimpered Cronin. "I haven't been mixed up in as many of these jobs as you have and is it surprising that I'm a mite nervous? It's no sign that I'm crawling."

"You're ready to stick it out, then?"

"Sure!"

There was another pause.

"Well, let me just tell you this, Jim Cronin. If you swear to stand by me and don't do it, your miserable life won't be worth a farthing—understand? I'll wring your neck, wring it good and thorough. I'm not afraid to do it and I will. You know that, don't you?"

"Yes."

The terror-stricken monosyllable made it perfectly apparent that Cronin did know.

"Then suppose we get down to hard tacks," asserted his companion, the note of fierceness suddenly dying out of his tone. "Come and sit down and we'll plan the thing from start to finish. We may as well be comfortable while we talk. There's no extra charge for sitting."

As Ted bent to put his ear to the crack of the door, the thud of a heavy body jarred the shack.

"Jove!" he heard Cronin cry. "The ground is some way down, ain't it?"

"And it's none to soft at that," came grimly from his comrade, as a second person slumped upon the planks outside.

Somebody drew a long breath and while the men were making themselves more comfortable on the float Ted waited expectantly in the darkness.

CHAPTER XIII

WHAT TED HEARD

"Now the question is which way are we going to get the biggest results," Alf began, when they were both comfortably settled with their backs to the door. "That must be the thing that governs us—that, and the sacrifice of as few lives as possible. Not their lives, of course. I don't care a curse for the Fernalds; the more of them that go sky-high the better, in my estimation. It's the men I mean, our own people. Some of them will have to die, I know that. It's unavoidable, since the factories are never empty. Even when no night shifts are working, there are always watchmen and engineers on the job. But fortunately just now, owing to the dull season, there are no night gangs on duty. If we decide on the mills it can be done at night; if on the Fernalds themselves, why we can set the bombs when we are sure that they are in their houses."

Ted bit his lips to suppress the sudden exclamation of horror that rose to them. He must not cry out, he told himself. Terrible as were the words he heard, unbelievable as they seemed, if he were to be of any help at all he must know the entire plot. Therefore he listened dumbly, struggling to still the beating of his heart.

For a moment there was no response from Cronin.

"Come, Jim, don't sit there like a graven image!" the leader of the proposed expedition exclaimed impatiently. "Haven't you a tongue in your head? What's your idea? Out with it. I'm not going to shoulder all the job."

The man called Cronin cleared his throat.

"As I see it, we gain nothing by blowing up the Fernald houses," answered he deliberately. "So long as the mills remain, their income is sure. After they're gone, the young one will just rebuild and go on wringing money out of the people as his father and grandfather are doing."

"But we mean to get him, too."

A murmured protest came from Cronin.

"I'm not for injuring that poor, unlucky lad," asserted he. "He's nothing but a cripple who can't help himself. It would be like killing a baby."

"Nonsense! What a sentimental milksop you are, Jim!" Alf cut in. "You can't go letting your feelings run away with you like that, old man. I'm sorry for the young chap, too. He's the most decent one of the lot. But that isn't the point. He's a Fernald and because he is——"

"But he isn't to blame for that, is he?"

"You make me tired, Cronin, with all this cry-baby stuff!" Alf ejaculated. "You've simply got to cut it out—shut your ears to it—if we are ever to accomplish anything. You can't let your sympathies run away with you like this."

"I ain't letting my sympathies run away with me," objected Cronin, in a surly tone. "And I'm no milksop, either. But I won't be a party to harming that unfortunate Mr. Laurie and you may as well understand that at the outset. I'm willing to do my share in blowing the Fernald mills higher than a kite, and the two Fernalds with 'em; or I'll blow the two Fernalds to glory in their beds. I could do it without turning a hair. But to injure that helpless boy of theirs I can't and won't. That would be too low-down a deed for me, bad as I am. He hasn't the show the others have. They can fend for themselves."

"You make me sick!" replied Alf scornfully. "Why, you might as well throw up the whole job as to only half do it. What use will it be to take the old men of the family if the young one still lives on?"

"I ain't going to argue with you, Alf," responded Cronin stubbornly. "If I were to talk all night you likely would never see my point. But there I stand and you can take it or leave it. If you want to go on on these terms, well and good; if not, I wash my hands of the whole affair and you can find somebody else to help you."

"Of course I can't find somebody else," was the exasperated retort. "You know that well enough. Do you suppose I would go on with a scheme like this and leave you wandering round to blab broadcast whatever you thought fit?"

"I shouldn't blab, Alf," declared Cronin. "You could trust me to hold my tongue and not peach on a pal. I should just pull out, that's all. I warn you, though, that if our ways parted and you went yours, I should do what I could to keep Mr. Laurie out of your path."

"You'd try the patience of Job, Cronin."

"I'm sorry."

"No, you're not," snarled Alf. "You're just doing this whole thing to be cussed. You know you've got me where I can't stir hand or foot. I was a fool ever to have got mixed up with such a white-livered, puling baby. I might have known you hadn't an ounce of sand."

"Take care, Sullivan," cautioned Cronin in a low, tense voice.

"But hang it all—why do you want to balk and torment me so?"

"I ain't balking and tormenting you."

"Yes, you are. You're just pulling the other way from sheer contrariness. Why can't you be decent and come across?"

"Haven't I been decent?" Cronin answered. "Haven't I fallen in with every idea you've suggested? You've had your way fully and freely. I haven't stood out for a single thing but this, have I?"

"N—o. But——"

"Well, why not give in and let me have this one thing as I want it? It don't amount to much, one way or the other. The boy is sickly and isn't likely to live long at best."

"But I can't for the life of me see why you should be so keen on sparing him. What is he to you?"

Cronin hesitated; then in a very low voice he said:

"Once, two years ago, my little kid got out of the yard and unbeknown to his mother wandered down by the river. We hunted high and low for him and were well-nigh crazy, for he's all the child we have, you know. It seems Mr. Laurie was riding along the shore in his automobile and he spied the baby creeping out on the thin ice. He stopped his car and called to the little one and coaxed him back until the chauffeur could get to him and lift him aboard the car. Then they fetched the child to the village, hunted up where he lived, and brought him home to his mother. I—I've never forgotten it and I shan't."

"That was mighty decent of Mr. Laurie—mighty decent," Sullivan admitted slowly. "I've got a kid at home myself."

For a few moments neither man spoke; then Sullivan continued in quick, brisk fashion, as if he were trying to banish some reverie that plagued him:

"Well, have your way. We'll leave Mr. Laurie out of this altogether."

"Thank you, Alf."

Sullivan paid no heed to the interruption.

"Now let's can all this twaddle and get down to work," he said sharply. "We've wasted too much time squabbling over that miserable cripple. Let's brace up and make our plans. You are for destroying the mills, eh?"

"It's the only thing that will be any use, it seems to me," Cronin replied. "If the mills are blown up, it will not only serve as a warning to the Fernalds but it will mean the loss of a big lot of money. They will rebuild, of course, but it will take time, and in the interval everything will be at a standstill."

"It will throw several hundred men out of work," Sullivan objected.

"That can't be helped," retorted Cronin. "They will get out at least with their lives and will be almighty thankful for that. They can get other jobs, I guess. But even if they are out of work, I figure some of them won't be so sorry to see the Fernalds get what's coming to them," chuckled Cronin.

"You're right there, Jim!"

"I'll bet I am!" cried Cronin.

"Then your notion would be to plant time bombs at the factories so they will go off in the night?"

"Yes," confessed Cronin, a shadow of regret in his tone. "That will carry off only a few watchmen and engineers. Mighty tough luck for them."

"It can't be helped," Sullivan said ruthlessly. "You can't expect to carry through a thing of this sort without some sacrifice. All we can do is to believe that the end justifies the means. It's a case of the greatest good to the greatest number."

"I—suppose—so."

"Well, then, why hesitate?"

"I ain't hesitating," announced Cronin quickly. "I just happened to remember Maguire. He's one of the night watchmen at the upper mill and a friend of mine."

"But we can't remember him, Cronin," Sullivan burst out. "It is unlucky that he chances to be on duty, of course; but that is his misfortune. We'd spare him if we could."

"I know, I know," Cronin said. "It's a pitiless business." Then, as if his last feeble compunction vanished with the words, he added, "It's to be the mills, then."

"Yes. We seem to be agreed on that," Sullivan replied eagerly. "I have everything ready and I don't see why we can't go right ahead to-night and plant the machines with their fuses timed for early morning. I guess we can sneak into the factories all right—you to the upper mill and I to the lower. If you get caught you can say you are hunting for Maguire; and if I do—well, I must trust to my wits to invent a story. But they won't catch me. I've never been caught yet, and I have handled a number of bigger jobs than this one," concluded he with pride.

"Anything more you want to say to me?" asked Cronin.

"No, I guess not. I don't believe I need to hand you any advice. Just stiffen up, that's all. Anything you want to say to me?"

"No. I shan't worry my head about you, you old fox. You're too much of a master hand," Cronin returned, with an inflection that sounded like a grin. "I imagine you can hold up your end."

"I rather imagine I can," drawled Sullivan.

"Then if there's nothing more to be said, I move we start back to town. It must be late," Cronin asserted.

"It's black enough to be midnight," grumbled Sullivan. "We'd best go directly to our houses—I to mine and you to yours. The explosives and bombs I'll pack into two grips. Yours I'll hide in your back yard underneath that boat. How'll that be?"

"O. K."

"You've got it straight in your head what you are to do?"

"Yes."

"And I can count on you?"

"Sure!"

"Then let's be off."

There was a splash as the canoe slipped into the water and afterward Ted heard the regular dip of the paddles as the craft moved away. He listened until the sound became imperceptible and when he was certain that the conspirators were well out of earshot he sped to the telephone and called up the police station at Freeman's Falls. It did not take long for him to hurriedly repeat to an officer what he had heard. Afterward, in order to make caution doubly sure, he called up the mills and got his old friend Maguire at the other end of the line. It was not until all this had been done and he could do no more that he sank limply down on the couch and stared into the darkness. Now that everything was over he found that he was shaking like a leaf. His hands were icy cold and he quivered in every muscle of his body. It was useless for him to try to sleep; he was far too excited and worried for that. Therefore he lay rigidly on his bunk, thinking and waiting for—he knew not what.

It might have been an hour later that he was aroused from a doze by the sharp reverberation of the telephone bell. Dizzily he sprang to his feet and stood stupid and inert in the middle of the floor. Again the signal rang and this time he was broad awake. He rushed forward to grasp the receiver.

"Turner? Ted Turner?"

"Yes, sir."

"This is the police station at Freeman's Falls. We have your men—both of them—and the goods on them. They are safe and sound under lock and key. I just thought you might like to know it. We shall want to see you in the morning. You've done a good night's work, young one. The State Police have been after these fellows for two years. Sullivan has a record for deeds of this sort. Mighty lucky we got a line on him this time before he did any mischief."

"It was."

"That's all, thanks to you, kid. I advise you to go to bed now and to sleep. I'll hunt you up to-morrow. I'll bet the Fernalds will, too. They owe you something."

CHAPTER XIV

THE FERNALDS WIN THEIR POINT

The trial of Alf Sullivan and Jim Cronin was one of the most spectacular and thrilling events Freeman's Falls had ever witnessed. That two such notorious criminals should have been captured through the efforts of a young boy was almost inconceivable to the police, especially to the State detectives whom they had continually outwitted. And yet here they were in the dock and the town officers made not the slightest pretense that any part of the glory of their apprehension belonged to them. To Ted Turner's prompt action, and to that alone, the triumph was due.

In consequence the boy became the hero of the village. He had always been a favorite with both young and old, for every one liked his father, and it followed that they liked his father's son. Now, however, they had greater cause to admire that son for his own sake and cherish toward him the warmest gratitude. Many a man and woman reflected that it was this slender boy who had stood between them and a calamity almost too horrible to be believed; and as a result their gratitude was tremendous. And if the townsfolk were sensible of this great obligation how much more keenly alive to it were the Fernalds whose property had been thus menaced.

"You have topped one service with another, Ted," Mr. Lawrence Fernald declared. "We do not see how we are ever to thank you. Come, there must be something that you would like—some wish you would be happy to have gratified. Tell us what it is and perhaps we can act as magicians and make it come true."

"Yes," pleaded Mr. Clarence Fernald, "speak out, Ted. Do not hesitate. Remember you have done us a favor the magnitude of which can never be measured and which we can never repay."

"But I do not want to be paid, sir," the lad answered. "I am quite as thankful as you that the wretches who purposed harm were caught before they had had opportunity to destroy either life or property. Certainly that is reward enough."

"It *is* a reward in its way," the elder Mr. Fernald asserted. "The thought that it was you who were the savior of an entire community will bring you happiness as long as you live. Nevertheless we should like to give you something more tangible than pleasant thoughts. We want you to have something by which to remember this marvelous escape from tragedy. Deep down in your heart there must be some wish you cherish. If you knew the satisfaction it would give us to gratify it, I am sure you would not be so reluctant to express it."

Ted colored, and after hesitating an instant, shyly replied:

"Since you are both so kind and really seem to wish to know, there is something I should like."

"Name it!" the Fernalds cried in unison.

"I should like to feel I can return to the shack next summer," the boy remarked timidly. "You see, I have become very fond of Aldercliffe and Pine Lea, fond of Laurie, of Mr. Hazen, and of the little hut. I have felt far more sorry than perhaps you realize to go away from here." His voice quivered.

"You poor youngster!" Mr. Clarence exclaimed. "Why in the name of goodness didn't you say so? There is no more need of your leaving this place than there is of my going, or Laurie. We ought to have sensed your feeling and seen to it that other plans were made long ago. Indeed, you shall come back to your little riverside abode next summer—never fear! And as for Aldercliffe, Pine Lea, Laurie and all the rest of it, you shall not be parted from any of them."

"But I must go back to school now, sir."

"What's the matter with your staying on at Pine Lea and having your lessons with Laurie and Mr. Hazen instead?"

"Oh—why——"

"Should you like to?"

"Oh, Mr. Fernald, it would be——"

Laurie's father laughed.

"I guess we do not need an answer to that question," Grandfather Fernald remarked, smiling. "His face tells the tale."

"Then the thing is as good as done," Mr. Clarence announced. "Hazen will be as set up as an old hen to have two chicks. He likes you, Ted."

"And well he may," growled Grandfather Fernald. "But for Ted's prayers and pleas he would not now be here."

"Yes, Hazen will be much pleased," reiterated Mr. Clarence Fernald, ignoring his father's comment. "As for Laurie—I wonder we never thought of all this before. It is no more work to teach two boys than one, and in the meantime each will act as a stimulus for the other. The spur of rivalry will be a splendid incentive for Laurie, to say nothing of the joy he will take in your companionship. He needs young people about him. It is a great scheme, a great scheme!" mused Mr. Fernald, rubbing his hands with increasing satisfaction as one advantage of the arrangement after another rotated through his mind.

"If only my father does not object," murmured Ted.

"Object! Object!" blustered Grandfather Fernald. "And why, pray, should he object?"

That a man of Mr. Turner's station in life should view the plan with anything but pride and complacency was evidently a new thought to the financier.

"Why, sir, my father and sisters are very fond of me and may not wish to have me remain longer away from home. They have missed me a lot this summer, I know that. You see I am the youngest one, the only boy."

"Humph!" interpolated the elder Mr. Fernald.

"In spite of the fact that we are crowded at home and too busy to see much of one another, Father likes to feel I'm around," continued Ted.

"I—suppose—so," came slowly from the old gentleman.

"I am sure I can fix all that," asserted Mr. Clarence Fernald briskly. "I will see your father and sisters myself, and I feel sure they will not stand in the way of your getting a fine education when it is offered you—that is, if they care as much for you as you say they do. On the contrary, they will be the first persons to realize that such a plan is greatly to your advantage."

"It is going to be almightily to your advantage," Mr. Lawrence Fernald added. "Who can tell where it all may lead? If you do well at your studies, perhaps it may mean college some day, and a big, well-paid job afterward."

Ted's eyes shone.

"Would you like to go to college if you could?" persisted the elder man.

"You bet I would—I mean yes, sir."

The old gentleman chuckled at the fervor of the reply.

"Well, well," said he, "time must decide all that. First lay a good foundation. You cannot build anything worth building without something to build upon. You get your cellar dug and we will then see what we will put on top of it."

With this parting remark he and his son moved away.

When the project was laid before Laurie, his delight knew no bounds. To have Ted come and live at Pine Lea for the winter, what a lark! Think of having some one to read and study with every day! Nothing could be jollier! And Mr. Hazen was every whit as pleased.

"It is the very thing!" he exclaimed to Laurie's father. "Ted will not be the least trouble. He is a fine student and it will be a satisfaction to work with him. Besides, unless I greatly miss my guess, he will cheer Laurie on to much larger accomplishments. Ted's influence has never been anything but good."

And what said Laurie's mother?

"It is splendid, Clarence, splendid! We can refurnish that extra room that adjoins Laurie's suite and let Mr. Hazen and the boys have that entire wing of the house. Nothing could be simpler. I shall be glad to have Ted here. Not only is he a fine boy but he has proved himself a good friend to us all. If we can do anything for him, we certainly should do it. The lad has had none too easy a time in this world."

Yes, all went well with the plan so far as the Fernalds were concerned; but the Turners—ah, there was the stumbling block!

"It's no doubt a fine thing you're offering to do for my son," Ted's father replied to Mr. Clarence Fernald, "and I assure you I am not unmindful of your kindness; but you see he is our only boy and when he isn't here whistling round the house we miss him. 'Tain't as if we had him at home during his vacation. If he goes up to your place to work summers and stays there winters as well, we shall scarcely see him at all. All we have had of him this last year was an occasional teatime visit. Folks don't like having their children go out from the family roof so young."

"But, Father," put in Nancy, "think what such a chance as this will mean to Ted. You yourself have said over and over again that there was nothing like having an education."

"I know it," mused the man. "There's nothing can equal knowing something. I never did and look where I've landed. I'll never go ahead none. But I want it to be different with my boy. He's going to have some stock in trade in the way of training for life. It will be a kind of capital nothing can sweep away. As I figure it, it will be a sure investment—that is, if the boy has any stuff in him."

"An education is a pretty solid investment," agreed the elder Mr. Fernald, "and you are wise to recognize its value, Mr. Turner. To plunge into life without such a weapon is like entering battle without a sword. I know, for I have tried it."

"Have you indeed, sir?"

Grandfather Fernald nodded.

"I was brought up on a Vermont farm when I was a boy."

"You don't say so! Well, well!"

"Yes, I never had much schooling," went on the old man. "Of course I picked up a lot of practical knowledge, as a boy will; and in some ways it has not been so bad. But it was a pretty mixed-up lot of stuff and I have been all my life sorting it out and putting it in order. I sometimes wonder when I think things over that I got ahead at all; it was more happen than anything else, I guess."

"The Vermonters have good heads on their shoulders," Mr. Turner remarked.

"Oh, you can't beat the Green Mountain State," laughed the senior Mr. Fernald, unbending into cordiality in the face of a common interest. "Still, when it came to bringing up my boy I felt as you do. I wasn't satisfied to have him get nothing more than I had. So I sent him to college and gave him all the education I never got myself. It has stood him in good stead, too, and I've lived to be proud of what he's done with it."

"And well you may be, sir," Mr. Turner observed.

Mr. Clarence Fernald flushed in the face of these plaudits and cut the conversation short by saying:

"It is that kind of an education that we want to give your boy, Mr. Turner. We like the youngster and believe he has promise of something fine. We should like to prepare him for college or some technical school and send him through it. He has quite a pronounced bent for science and given the proper opportunities he might develop into something beyond the ordinary rank and file."

"Do you think so, sir?" asked Mr. Turner, glowing with pleasure. "Well, I don't know but that he has a sort of knack with wire, nails, and queer machinery. He has tinkered with such things since he was a little lad. Of late he has been fussing round with electricity and scaring us all to death here at home. His sisters were always expecting he'd meet his end or blow up the house with some claptraption he'd put together."

Nancy blushed; then added, with a shy glance toward the Fernalds:

"They say down at the school that Ted is quite handy with telephones and such things."

"Mr. Hazen, my son's tutor, thinks your brother has a knowledge of electricity far beyond his years," replied Mr. Clarence Fernald. "That is why it seems a pity his talents in that direction should not be cultivated. Who knows but he may be an embryo genius? You never can tell what may be inside a child."

"You're right there, sir," Mr. Turner assented cordially. Then after a moment of thought, he continued, "Likely an education such as you are figuring on would cost a mint of money."

The Fernalds, both father and son, smiled at the naïve comment.

"Well—yes," confessed Mr. Clarence slowly. "It would cost something."

"A whole lot?"

"If you wanted the best."

Mr. Turner scratched his head.

"I'm afraid I couldn't swing it," declared he, regret in his tone.

"But we are offering to do this for you," put in Grandfather Fernald.

"I know you are, sir; I know you are and I'm grateful," Ted's father answered. "But if I could manage it myself, I'd——"

"Come, Mr. Turner, I beg you won't say that," interrupted the elder Mr. Fernald. "Think what we owe to your son. Why, we never in all the world can repay what he has done for us. This is no favor. We are simply paying our debts. You like to pay your bills, don't you?"

"Indeed I do, sir!" was the hearty reply. "There's no happier moment than the one when I take my pay envelope and go to square up what I owe. True, I don't run up many bills; still, there is not always money enough on hand to make both ends meet without depending some on credit."

"How much do you get in the shipping room?"

"Eighty dollars a month, sir."

"And your daughters are working?"

"They are in the spinning mills."

Mr. Fernald glanced about over the little room. Although scrupulously neat, it was quite apparent that the apartment was far too crowded for comfort. The furnishings also bespoke frugality in the extreme. It was not necessary to be told that the Turners' life was a close arithmetical problem.

"Your family stand by us loyally," observed the financier.

"We have your mills to thank for our daily bread, sir," Mr. Turner answered.

"And your boy—if he does not go on with his studies shall you have him enter the factories?"

Mr. Turner squared his shoulders with a swift gesture of protest.

"No, sir—not if I can help it!" he burst out. Then as if he suddenly sensed his discourtesy, he added, "I beg your pardon, gentlemen. I wasn't thinking who I was talking to. It isn't that I do not like the mills. It's only that there is so little chance for the lad to get ahead there. I wouldn't want the boy to spend his life grubbing away as I have."

"And yet you are denying him the chance to better himself."

"I am kinder going round in a circle, ain't I?" returned Mr. Turner gently. "Like as not it is hard for you to understand how I feel. It's only that you hate to let somebody else do for your children. It seems like charity."

"Charity! Charity—when we owe the life of our boy, the lives of many of our workmen, the safety of our mills to your son?" ejaculated Mr. Clarence Fernald with unmistakable sincerity.

"When you pile it up that way it does sound like a pretty big debt, doesn't it?" mused Mr. Turner.

"Of course it's a big debt—it is a tremendous one. Now try, Mr. Turner, and see our point of view. We want to take our envelope in our hands and although we have not fortune enough in the world to wipe out all we owe, we wish to pay part of it, at least. No matter how much we may be able to do for Ted in the future, we shall never be paying in full all that he has done for us. Much of his service we must accept as an obligation and give in return for it nothing but gratitude and affection. But if you will grant us the privilege of doing this little, it will give us the greatest pleasure."

If any one had told the stately Mr. Lawrence Fernald weeks before that he would be in the home of one of his workmen, pleading for a favor, he would probably have shrugged his shoulders and laughed; and even Mr. Clarence Fernald, who was less of an aristocrat than his father, would doubtless have questioned a prediction of his being obliged actually to implore one of the men in his employ to accept a benefaction from him. Yet here they both were, almost upon their knees, theoretically, before this self-respecting artisan.

In the face of such entreaty who could have remained obdurate? Certainly not Mr. Turner who in spite of his pride was the kindest-hearted creature alive.

"Well, you shall have your way, gentlemen," he at length replied, "Ted shall stay on at Pine Lea, since you wish it, and you shall plan his education as you think best. I know little of such matters and feel sure the problem is better in your hands than mine. I know you will work for the boy's good. And I beg you won't think me ungrateful because I have hesitated to accept your offer. We all have our scruples and I have mine. But now that I have put them in the background, I shall take whole-heartedly what you give and be most thankful for it."

Thus did the Fernalds win their point. Nevertheless they came away from the Turner's humble home with a consciousness that instead of bestowing a favor, as they had expected to do, they had really received one. Perhaps they did not respect Ted's father the less because of his reluctance to take the splendid gift they had put within his reach. They themselves were proud men and they had a sympathy for the pride of others. There could be no question that the interview had furnished both of them with food for thought for as they drove home in their great touring car they did not speak immediately. By and by, however, Grandfather Fernald observed:

"Don't you think, Clarence, Turner's pay should be increased? Eighty dollars isn't much to keep a roof over one's head and feed a family of three persons."

"I have been thinking that, too," returned his son. "They tell me he is a very faithful workman and he has been here long enough to have earned a substantial increase in wages. I don't see why I never got round to doing something for him before. The fellow was probably too proud to ask for more money and unless some kick comes to me those things slip my mind. I'll see right away what can be done."

There was a pause and then the senior Mr. Fernald spoke again:

"Do you ever feel that we ought to do something about furnishing better quarters for the men?" he asked. "I have had the matter on my conscience for months. Look at that tenement of the Turners! It is old, out of date, crowded and stuffy. There isn't a ray of sunshine in it. It's a disgrace to herd a family into such a place. And I suppose there are ever so many others like it in Freeman's Falls."

"I'm afraid there are, Father."

"I don't like the idea of it," growled old Mr. Fernald. "The houses all look well enough until one goes inside. But they're terrible, terrible! Why, they are actually depressing. I haven't shaken off the gloom of that room yet. We own land enough on the other side of the river. Why couldn't we build a handsome bridge and then develop that unused area by putting up some decent houses for our people? It would increase the value of the property and at the same time improve the living conditions of our employees. What do you say to the notion?"

"I am ready to go in on any such scheme!" cried Mr. Clarence Fernald heartily. "I'd like nothing better. I have always wanted to take up the matter with you; but I fancied from something you said once when I suggested it that you——"

"I didn't realize what those houses down along the water front were like," interrupted Grandfather Fernald. "Ugh! At least sunshine does not cost money. We must see that our people get more of it."

CHAPTER XV

WHAT CAME OF THE PLOT

The Fernalds were as good as their word. All winter long father, son, and grandson worked at the scheme for the new cottages and by New Year, with the assistance of an architect, they had on paper plans for a model village to be built on the opposite side of the river as soon as the weather permitted. The houses were gems of careful thought, no two of them being alike. Nevertheless, although each tiny domain was individual in design, a general uniformity of construction existed between them which resulted in a delightfully harmonious ensemble. The entire Fernald family was enthusiastic over the project. It was the chief topic of conversation both at Aldercliffe and at Pine Lea. Rolls of blue prints littered office and library table and cluttered the bureaus, chairs, and even the pockets of the elder men of each household.

"We are going to make a little Normandy on the other shore of the river before we have done with it," asserted Grandfather Fernald to Laurie. "It will be as pretty a settlement as one would wish to see. I mean, too, to build cooperative stores, a clubhouse, and a theater; perhaps I may even go farther and put up a chapel. I have gone clean daft over the notion of a model village and since I am started I may as well be hung for a sheep as a lamb. I do not believe we shall be sinking our money, either, for in addition to bettering the living conditions of our men I feel we shall also draw to the locality a finer class of working people. This will boom our section of the country and should make property here more valuable. But even if it doesn't work out that way, I shall take pride in the proposed village. I have always insisted that our mills be spotless and up to date and the fact that they have been has been a source of great gratification. Now I shall carry that idea farther and see that the new settlement comes up to our standards. I have gone over and over the plans to see if in any way they can be bettered; suppose you and I look at them together once more. Some new inspiration may come to us—something that will be an improvement."

Patiently and for the twentieth time Laurie examined the blue prints while his grandfather volubly explained just where each building of the many was to stand.

"This little park, with a fountain in the middle and a band-stand near by, will slope down toward the river. As there are many fine trees along the shore it will be a cool and pleasant place to sit in summer. The stone bridge I am to put up will cross just above and serve as a sort of entrance to the park. We intend that everything shall be laid out with a view to making the river front attractive. As for the village itself—the streets are to be wide so that each dwelling shall have plenty of fresh air and sunshine. No more of those dingy flats such as the Turners live in! Each family is also to have land enough for a small garden, and each house will have a piazza and the best of plumbing; and because many of the women live in their kitchens more than in any other part of their abode, I am insisting that that room be as comfortable and airy as it can be made."

"It is all bully, Grandfather," Laurie answered. "But isn't it going to cost a fortune to do the thing as you want it done?"

"It is going to cost money," nodded the elder man. "I am not deceiving myself as to that. But I have the money and if I chose to spend it on this *fad* (as one of my friends called it) I don't see why I shouldn't do it. Since your grandmother died I have not felt the same interest in Aldercliffe that I used to. When she was alive that was my hobby. I shall simply be putting out the money in a different direction, that is all. Perhaps it will be a less selfish direction, too."

"It certainly is a bully fine fad, Grandfather," Laurie exclaimed.

"Somehow I believe it is, laddie," the old gentleman answered thoughtfully. "Your father thinks so. Time only can tell whether I have chucked my fortune in a hole or really invested it wisely. I have been doing a good deal of serious thinking lately, thanks to those chaps who tried to blow up the mills. As I have turned matters over in my mind since the trial, and struggled to get their point of view, I have about come to the conclusion that they had a fair measure of right on their side. Not that I approve of their methods," continued he hastily, raising a protesting hand, when Laurie offered an angry interruption. "Do not misunderstand me. The means they took was cowardly and criminal and I do not for a moment uphold it. But the thing that led them to act as they planned to act was that they honestly believed we had not given them and their comrades a square deal. As I have pondered over this conviction of theirs, I am not so sure but they were right in that belief."

He paused to light a fresh cigar which he silently puffed for a few moments.

"This village plan of mine has grown to some extent out of the thinking to which this tragedy has stimulated me. There can be no question that our fortunes have come to us as a result of the hard labor of our employees. I know that. And I also know that we have rolled up a far larger proportion of the profits than they have. In fact, I am not sure we have not accepted a larger slice than was our due; and I am not surprised that some of them are also of that opinion. I would not go so far as to say we have been actually dishonest but I am afraid we have not been generous. The matter never came to me before in precisely this light and I confess frankly I am sorry that I have blundered. Nevertheless, as I tell your father, it is never too late to mend. If we have made mistakes we at least do not need to continue to make them. So I have resolved to pay up some of my past obligations by building this village and afterward your dad and I plan to raise the wages of the workers—raise them voluntarily without their asking. I figure we shall have enough to keep the wolf from the door, even then," he added, smiling, "and if we should find we had not, why we should simply have to come back on you and Ted Turner to support us, that's all."

Laurie broke into a ringing laugh.

"I would much rather you and Dad spent the money this way than to have you leave it all to me," he said presently.

"One person does not need so much money. It is more than his share of the world's profits—especially if he has earned none of it. Besides, when a fortune is handed over to you, it spoils all the fun of making one for yourself." The boy's eyes clouded wistfully. "I suppose anyhow I never shall be able to work as hard as you and Father have; still I———"

"Pooh! Pooh! Nonsense!" his grandfather interrupted huskily.

"I believe I shall be able to earn enough to take care of myself," continued Laurie steadily. "In any case I mean to try."

"Of course you will!" cried the elder man heartily. "Why, aren't you expecting to be an engineer or something?"

"I—I—hope—to," replied the boy.

"Certainly! Certainly!" fidgeted Grandfather Fernald nervously. "You are going to be a great man some day, Laurie—a consulting engineer, maybe; or a famous electrician, or something of the sort."

"I wish I might," the lad repeated. "You see, Grandfather, it is working out your own career that is the fun, making something all yourself. That is why I hate the idea of ever stepping into your shoes and having to manage the mills. All the interesting part is done already. You and Dad had the pleasure——"

"The damned hard work, you mean," cut in his grandfather.

"Well, the hard work, then," chuckled Laurie, "of building the business up."

"That is true, my boy," replied Mr. Fernald. "It was a great game, too. Why, you know when I came here and we staked out the site for the mills, there wasn't a house in sight. There was nothing but that river. To one little wooden factory and that rushing torrent of water I pinned my faith. Every cent I possessed in the world was in the venture. I must make good or go under. Nobody will ever know how I slaved in those early days. For years I worked day and night, never giving myself time to realize that I was tired. But I was young and eager and although I got fagged sometimes a few hours of sleep sent me forth each morning with faith that I could slay whatever dragons I might encounter. As I look back on those years, hard though they were, they will always stand out as the happiest ones of my life. It was the fight that was the sport. Now I am an old man and I have won the thing I was after—success. Of course, it is a satisfaction to have done what you set out to do. But I tell you, laddie, that after your money is made, the zest of the game is gone. Your fortune rolls up then without you and all you have to do is to sit back and watch it grow of itself. It doesn't seem to be a part of you any more. You feel old, and unnecessary, and out of it. You are on the shelf."

"That is why I want to begin at the beginning and earn my own money, Grandfather," Laurie put in. "Think what you would have missed if some one had deprived you of all your fun when you were young. You wouldn't have liked it."

"You bet I wouldn't!" cried the old gentleman.

"I don't want to lose my fun either," persisted Laurie. "I want to win my way just as you and Dad have done—just as Ted Turner is going to do. I want to find out what is in me and what I can do with it."

Grandfather Fernald rubbed his hands.

"Bully for you, Laurie! Bully for you!" he ejaculated. "That's the true Fernald spirit. It was that stuff that took me away from my father's farm in Vermont and started me out in the world with only six dollars in my pocket. I was bound I would try my muscle and I did. I got some pretty hard knocks, too, while I was doing it. Still, they were all in the day's work and I never have regretted them. But I didn't mean to have your father go through all I did and so I saw that he got an education and started different. He knew what he was fighting and was armed with the proper weapons instead of going blind into the scrimmage. That is what we are trying to do for you and what we mean to do for Ted Turner. We do not intend to take either of you out of the fray but we are going to put into your hands the things you need to win the battle. Then the making good will depend solely on you."

"I mean to try to do my part."

"I know you do, laddie; and you'll do it, too."

"I just wish I was stronger—as well as Ted is," murmured the boy.

"I wish you were," his grandfather responded gently, touching his grandson's shoulder affectionately with his strong hand. "If money could give you health you should have every farthing I possess. But there are things that money cannot do, Laurie. I used to think it was all-powerful and that if I had it there was nothing I could not make mine. But I realize now that many of the best gifts of life are beyond its reach. We grow wiser as we grow older," he concluded, with a sad shake of his head. "Sometimes I think we should have been granted two lives, one to experiment with and the other to live."

He rose, a weary shadow clouding his eyes.

"Well, to live and learn is all we can do; and thank goodness it is never too late to profit by our errors. I have learned many things from Ted Turner; I have learned some more from his father; and I have added to all these certain things that those unlucky wretches, Sullivan and Cronin, have demonstrated to me. Who knows but I may make Freeman's Falls a better place in consequence? We shall see."

With these parting reflections the old gentleman slowly left the room.

CHAPTER XVI

ANOTHER CALAMITY

The winter was a long and tedious one with much cold weather and ice. Great drifts leveled the fields about Aldercliffe and Pine Lea, shrouding the vast expanse of fields along the river in a glistening cloak of ermine spangled with gold. The stream itself was buried so deep beneath the snow that it was difficult not to believe it had disappeared altogether. Freeman's Falls had never known a more severe season and among the mill employees there was much illness and depression. Prices were high, business slack, and the work ran light. Nevertheless, the Fernalds refused to shorten the hours. There were no night shifts on duty, to be sure, but the hum of the machinery that ceased at twilight resumed its buzzing every morning and by its music gladdened many a home where anxiety might otherwise have reigned.

That the factories were being operated at a loss rather than throw the men out of employment Ted Turner could not help knowing, for since he had become a member of the Fernald household he had been included so intimately in the family circle that it was unavoidable he should be cognizant of much that went on there. As a result, an entirely new aspect of manufacture came before him. Up to this time he had seen but one side of the picture, that with which the working man was familiar.

152

But now the capitalist's side was turned toward him and on confronting its many intricate phases he gained a very different conception of the mill-owner's conundrums. He learned now for the first time who it was that tided over business in its seasons of stress and advanced the money that kept bread in the mouths of the workers. He sensed, too, as he might never have done otherwise, who shouldered the burden of care not alone during working hours but outside of them; he glimpsed something of the struggles of competition; the problems of securing raw material; the work concerning credits.

A very novel viewpoint it was to the boy, and as he regarded the complicated web, he found himself wondering how much of all this tangle was known to the men, and whether they were always fair to their employer. He had frequently overheard conversations at his father's when they had proclaimed how easy and care-free a life the rich led, and while they had envied and criticized and slandered the Fernalds and asserted that they did nothing but enjoy themselves, he had listened. Ah, how far from the truth this estimate had been! He speculated, as he reviewed the facts and vaguely rehearsed the capitalist's enigmas whether, if shown the actual conditions, the townsfolk would have been willing to exchange places with either of these men whose fortunes they so greedily coveted.

For in very truth the Fernalds seemed to Ted persons to be pitied far more than envied. Stripped of illusions, what was Mr. Lawrence Fernald but an old man who had devoted himself to money-making until he had rolled up a fortune so large that its management left him no leisure to enjoy it? Eager to accumulate more and ever more wealth, he toiled and worried quite as hard as he would have done had he had no money at all; he often passed sleepless nights and could never be persuaded to take a day away from his office. He slaved harder than any of those he paid to work for him and he had none of their respite from care.

Mr. Clarence Fernald, being of a younger generation, had perhaps learned greater wisdom. At any rate, he went away twice a year for extended pleasure trips. Possibly the fact that his father had degenerated into a mere money-making machine was ever before him, serving as a warning against a similar fate. However that may have been, he did break resolutely away from business at intervals, or tried to. Nevertheless, he never could contrive to be wholly free. Telegrams pursued him wherever he went; his secretary often went in search of him; and many a time, like a defeated runaway whose escape is cut short, he was compelled to abandon his holiday and return to the mills, there to straighten out some unlooked-for complication. Day and night the responsibilities of his position, the welfare of the hundreds of persons dependent on him, weighed down his shoulders. And even when he was at home in the bosom of his family, there was Laurie, his son, his idol, who could probably never be well! What man in all Freeman's Falls could have envied him if acquainted with all the conditions of his life?

This and many another such reflection engrossed Ted, causing him to wonder whether there was not in the divine plan a certain element of equalization.

In the meantime, his lessons with Laurie and Mr. Hazen went steadily and delightfully on. How much more could be accomplished with a tutor who devoted all his time simply to two pupils! And how much greater pleasure one derived from studying under these intimate circumstances! In every way the arrangement was ideal. Thus the winter passed with its balancing factors of work and play. The friendship between the two boys strengthened daily and in a similar proportion Ted's affection for the entire Fernald family increased.

It was when the first thaw made its appearance late in March that trouble came. Laurie was stricken with measles, and because of the contagion, Ted's little shack near the river was hastily equipped for occupancy, and the lad was transferred there.

"I can't have two boys sick," declared Mr. Clarence Fernald, "and as you have not been exposed to the disease there is no sense in our thrusting you into its midst. Plenty of wood will keep your fireplace blazing and as the weather is comparatively mild I fancy you can contrive to be comfortable. We will connect the telephone so you won't be lonely and so you can talk with Laurie every day. The doctor says he will soon be well again and after the house has been fumigated you can come back to Pine Lea."

Accordingly, Ted was once more ensconced in the little hut and how good it seemed to be again in that familiar haunt only he realized. Before the first day was over, he felt as if he had never been away. Pine Lea might boast its conservatories, its sun parlors, its tiled baths, its luxuries of every sort; they all faded into nothingness beside the freedom and peace of the tiny shack at the river's margin.

Meanwhile, with the gradual approach of spring, the sun mounted higher and the great snow drifts settled and began to disappear. Already the ice in the stream was breaking up and the turbid yellow waters went rushing along, carrying with them whirling blocks of snow. As the torrent swept past, it flooded the meadows and piled up against the dam opposite the factories great frozen, jagged masses of ice which ground and crashed against one another, so that the sounds could be distinctly heard within the mills. At some points these miniature icebergs blocked the falls and held the waters in check until, instead of cascading over the dam, they spread inland, inundating the shores. The float before Ted's door was covered and at night, when all was still and his windows open, he could hear the roaring of the stream, and the impact of the bumping ice as it sped along. Daily, as the snows on the far distant hillsides near the river's source melted, the flood increased and poured down in an ever rising tide its seething waters.

Yet notwithstanding the fact that each day saw the stream higher, no one experienced any actual anxiety from the conditions, although everybody granted they were abnormal. Of course, there was more ice in the river than there had been for many years. Even Grandfather Fernald, who had lived in the vicinity for close on to half a century, could not recall ever having witnessed such a spring freshet; nor did he deny that the weight of ice and water against the dam must be tremendous. However, the structure was strong and there was no question of its ability to hold, even though this chaos of grinding ice-cakes boomed against it with defiant reverberation.

In spite of the conditions, Ted felt no nervousness about remaining by himself in the shack and perhaps every premonition of evil might have escaped him had he not been awakened one morning very early by a ripple of lapping water that seemed near at hand. Sleepily he opened his eyes and looked about him. The floor of the hut was wet and through the crack beneath the door a thread of muddy water was steadily seeping. In an instant he was on his feet and as he stood looking about him in bewilderment he heard the roar of the river and detected in the sound a threatening intonation that had not been there on the previous day. He hurried to the window and stared out into the grayness of the dawn. The scene that confronted him chilled his blood. The river had risen unbelievably during the night. Not only were the little bushes along the shore entirely submerged but many of the pines standing upon higher ground were also under water.

As he threw on his clothes, he tried to decide whether there was anything he ought to do. Would it be well to call up the Fernalds, or telephone to the mills, or to the village, and give warning of the conditions? It was barely four o'clock and the first streaks of light were but just appearing. Nevertheless, there must be persons who were awake and as alert as he to the transformation the darkness had wrought. Moreover, perhaps there was no actual danger, and should this prove to be the case, how absurd he would feel to arouse people at daybreak for a mere nothing. It was while he paused there indecisively that a sight met his eye which spurred hesitancy to immediate action. Around the bend far up the stream came sweeping a tangle of wreckage—trees, and brush, and floating timber—and swirling along in its wake was a small lean-to which he recognized as one that had stood on the bank of the river at Melton, the village located five miles above Freeman's Falls. If the water were high enough to carry away this building, it must indeed have risen to a menacing height and there was not a moment to be lost.

He rushed to the telephone and called up Mr. Clarence Fernald who replied to his summons in irritable, half-dazed fashion.

"Is there any way of lifting the water gates at the mills?" asked Ted breathlessly. "The river has risen so high that it is sweeping away trees and even some of the smaller houses from the Melton shore. If the debris piles up against the dam, the pressure may be more than the thing can stand. Besides, the water will spread and flood both Aldercliffe and Pine Lea. I thought I'd better tell you."

Mr. Fernald was not dazed now; he was broad awake.

"Where are you?" inquired he sharply.

"At the shack, sir. The water is ankle deep."

"Don't stay there another moment. It is not safe. At any instant the whole hut may be carried away. Gather your traps together and call Wharton or Stevens—or both of them—to come and help you take them up to Aldercliffe. I'll attend to notifying the mills. You've done us a good turn, my boy."

During the next hour Ted himself was too busy to appreciate the hectic rush of events that he had set moving, or realize the feverish energy with which the Fernalds and their employees worked to avert a tragedy which, but for his warning, might have been a very terrible one. The mills were reached by wire and the sluices at the sides of the central dam immediately lifted to make way for the torrent of snow, ice, wreckage, and water. In what a fierce and maddened chaos it surged over the falls and dashed into the chasm beneath! All day the mighty current boiled and seethed, overflowing the outlying fields with its yellow flood. Nevertheless, the great brick factories that bordered the stream stood firm and so did the residences at Aldercliffe and Pine Lea, both of which were fortunately situated on high ground.

Ted had not made his escape from his little camp a moment too soon, for while he stood looking out on the freshet from one of the attic windows at Pine Lea, he shivered to behold his little hut bob past him amid the rushing waters and drift into an eddy on the opposite shore along with a mass of uprooted pines.

A sob burst from him.

"It's gone, Mr. Hazen—our little house!" he murmured brokenly to the young tutor who was standing beside him. "We never shall see it again."

"You mustn't take it so to heart, Ted," the teacher answered, laying his hand sympathetically on the lad's shoulder. "Suppose you had been in it and borne away to almost certain death. That would have been a calamity indeed. What is an empty boathouse when we consider how many people are to suffer actual financial loss and perhaps forfeit everything they have, as a result of this tragedy. The villagers who live along the river will lose practically everything they own—boats, poultry, barns; and many of them both houses and furniture. We all loved the shack; but it is not as if its destruction left you with no other roof above your head. You can stay at Aldercliffe, Pine Lea, or join your family at Freeman's Falls. Three shelters are open to you. But these poor souls in the town——"

"I had not thought about the villagers," blushed Ted.

"The Fernalds have been in the settlement since dawn and along with every man they could summon have been working to save life and property. If I had not had to stay here with Laurie, I should have gone to help, too."

Ted hung his head.

"I'm ashamed to have been so selfish," said he. "Instead of thinking only of myself, I ought to have been lending a hand to aid somebody else. It was rotten of me. Why can't I go down to the village now? There must be things I can do. Certainly I'm no use here."

"No, there is nothing to be done here," the tutor agreed. "If you could stay with Laurie and calm him down there would be some sense in your remaining; but as it is, I don't see why you shouldn't go along to the town and fill in wherever you can. I fancy there will be plenty to do. The Fernalds, Wharton, Stevens, and the rest of the men are moving the families who lived along the water front out of their houses and into others. All our trucks and cars are busy at the job."

"I know I could help," cried Ted eagerly, his foot on the top step of the staircase.

"I am sure you can," Mr. Hazen replied. "Already by your timely warning you have helped more than you will ever know. I tremble to think what might have happened if you had not awakened Mr. Clarence just when you did. Had the dam at the mills gone down, the whole town would have been devastated. Mr. Fernald told me so himself."

"I'm mighty glad if I———"

"So you see you have been far from selfish," continued the tutor, in a cheery tone. "As for the shack, it can be rebuilt, so I should not mourn about that."

"I guess Mr. Fernald is glad now that he has his plans ready for his model village."

"Yes, he is. He said right away that it was providential. The snow will disappear after this thaw and as soon as the earth dries up enough to admit of building, the workmen will begin to break ground for the new settlement. The prospect of other and better houses than the old ones will encourage many of the mill people who have had their dwellings ruined to-day and in consequence been forced to move into temporary quarters where they are crowded and uncomfortable. We can all endure inconvenience when we know it is not to last indefinitely. Mr. Fernald told me over the telephone that the promise of new houses by summer or fall at the latest was buoying up the courage of all those who had suffered from this terrible disaster. He is going to grant special privileges to every family that has met with loss. They are to be given the first houses that are finished."

"I do hope another freshet like this one won't sweep away the new village," reflected Ted.

"Oh, we shall probably never again be treated to an excitement similar to this one," smiled Mr. Hazen reassuringly. "Didn't you hear them say that it was the bursting of the Melton reservoir which was largely responsible for this catastrophe? Mr. Fernald declared all along that this was no ordinary freshet. He has seen the river every spring for nearly forty years and watched it through all its annual thaws; and although it has often been high, it has never been a danger to the community. He told me over the telephone about the reservoir bursting. He had just got the news. It seems the reservoir above Melton was an old one which the authorities have realized for some time must be rebuilt. They let it go one year too long. With the weight of water, snow, and ice, it could not bear the pressure put upon it and collapsed. I'm afraid it has been a severe lesson to the officials of the place for the chance they took has caused terrible damage."

"Were people killed?" asked Ted in an awed whisper.

"We have heard so—two or three who were trapped asleep in their houses. As for the town, practically all the buildings that fronted the river were destroyed. Of course, as yet we have not been able to get very satisfactory details, for most of the wires were down and communication was pretty well cut off. I suppose that is why they did not notify us of our peril. People were probably too busy with their own affairs, too intent on saving their own lives and possessions to think of anything else. Then, too, the thing came suddenly. If there hadn't been somebody awake here, I don't know where we should have been. I don't see how you happened to be astir so early."

"Nor I," returned Ted modestly. "I think it must have been the sound of the water coming in that woke me. I just happened to hear it."

"Well, it was an almighty fortunate happen—that is all I can say," asserted Mr. Hazen, as the boy sped down the stairs.

CHAPTER XVII

SURPRISES

During the next few days tidings of the Melton disaster proved the truth of Mr. Hazen's charitable suppositions, for it was definitely learned that the calamity which befell the village came entirely without warning, and as the main part of the town was wiped out almost completely and the river front destroyed, all communication between the unfortunate settlement and the outside world had been cut off so that to send warnings to the communities below had been impossible. Considering the enormity of the catastrophe, it was miraculous that there had not been greater loss of life and wider spread devastation.

A week of demoralization all along the river followed the tragedy; but after the bulk of wreckage was cleared away and the stream had dropped to normal, the Fernalds actually began to congratulate themselves on the direful event.

"Well, the thing has not been all to the bad, by any means," commented Grandfather Fernald. "We have at least got rid of those unsightly tenements bordering the water which were such a blot on Freeman's Falls; and once gone, I do not mean to allow them ever to be put back again. I have bought up the land and shall use it as the site of the new granite bridge I intend to build across the stream. And in case I have more land than is needed for this purpose, the extra area can be used for a park which will be an ornament to the spot rather than an eyesore. Therefore, take it altogether, I consider that freshet a capital thing."

He glanced at Ted who chanced to be standing near by.

"I suppose you, my lad, do not entirely agree with me," added he, a twinkle gleaming beneath his shaggy brows. "You are thinking of that playhouse of yours and Laurie's that was carried off by the deluge."

"I am afraid I was, sir."

"Pooh! Nonsense!" blustered the old gentleman. "What's a thing like that? Besides, Laurie's father proposes to rebuild it for you. Hasn't he told you?" questioned the man, noticing the surprise in the boy's face. "Oh, yes, indeed! He is going to put up another house for you; and judging from his plans, you will find yourself far better off than you were in the first place for this time he is to give you a real cottage, not simply a made-over boathouse. Yes, there is to be running water; a bedroom, study, and kitchenette; to say nothing of a bath and steam heat. He plans to connect it by piping with the central heating plant. So you see you will have a regular housekeeping bungalow instead of a camp."

Ted gasped.

"But—but—I can't let Mr. Fernald do all this for me," he protested. "It's—it's—too much."

"I shouldn't worry about him, if I were you," smiled the elder man. "It won't scrimp him, I imagine. Furthermore, it will be an excellent investment, for should the time ever come when you did not need the house it could be rented to one of our tenants. He is to put a foundation under it this time and build it more solidly; and possibly he may decide to set it a trifle farther back from the water. In any case, he will see that it is right; you can trust him for that. It will not be carried away a second time."

"I certainly hope not," Ted agreed. "What a pity it was they did not have some way of notifying us from Melton! If they had only had a wireless apparatus——" he broke off thoughtfully.

"I doubt if all the wireless in the world could have saved your little hut," answered Mr. Fernald kindly. "It was nothing but a pasteboard house and wireless or no wireless it would have gone anyway. I often speculate as to how ships ever dared to go to sea before they had the protection of wireless communication. Ignorance was bliss, I suppose. They knew nothing about it and therefore did not miss it. When we can boast no better way we are satisfied with the old. But think of the shipwrecks and accidents that might have been averted! You will be studying about all this some day when you go to Technology or college."

Ted's face lighted at the words.

"You have all been so kind to me, Mr. Fernald," he murmured. "When I think of your sending me to college it almost bowls me over."

"You must never look upon it as an obligation, my boy," the old gentleman declared. "If there is any obligation at all (and there is a very real one) it is ours. The only obligation you have will be to do well at your studies and make us proud of you, and that you are doing all the time. Mr. Hazen tells me you are showing splendid progress. I hope by another week Laurie will be out of the woods, Pine Lea will be fumigated, and you can resume your former way of living there without further interruptions from floods and illness. Still, I shall be sorry to have your little visit at Aldercliffe come to an end. You seem to have grown into the ways of the whole family and to fit in wherever you find yourself."

Mr. Fernald smiled affectionately at the lad.

"There is something that has been on my tongue's end to

whisper to you for some time," he went on, after a brief interval of hesitancy. "I know you can keep a secret and so I mean to tell you one. In the spring we are going to take Laurie over to New York to see a very celebrated surgeon who is coming from Vienna to this country. We hear he has had great success with cases such as Laurie's and we hope he may be able to do something for the boy. Of course, no one knows this as yet, not even Laurie himself."

"Oh, Mr. Fernald! Do you mean there would be a chance that Laurie could walk sometime?" Ted cried.

The old man looked into the young and shining face and nervously brushed the back of his hand across his eyes.

"Perhaps; perhaps!" responded he gruffly. "Who can tell? This doctor has certainly performed some marvelous cures. Who knows but the lad may some day not only walk about, but leap and run as you do!"

"Oh, sir—!"

"But we must not be too sure or allow ourselves to be swept away by hope," cautioned Grandfather Fernald. "No one knows what can be done yet and we might be disappointed—sadly disappointed. Still, there is no denying that there is a fighting chance. But keep this to yourself, Ted. I must trust you to do that. If Laurie were to know anything about it, it would be very unfortunate, for the ordeal will mean both pain and suffering for him and he must not be worried about it in advance. He will need all his nerve and courage when the time for action comes. Moreover, we feel it would be cruel for him to glimpse such a vision and then find it only a mirage. So we have told him nothing. But I have told you because you are fond of him and I wanted you to share the secret."

"It shall remain a secret, Mr. Fernald."

"I feel sure of that," the man replied. "You are a good boy, Ted. It was a lucky day that brought you to Pine Lea."

"A lucky one for me, sir!"

"For all of us, son! For all of us!" reiterated the old gentleman. "The year of your coming here will be one we never shall forget. It has been very eventful."

Certainly the final comment was no idle one. Not only had the year been a red-letter one but it was destined to prove even more conspicuously memorable. With the spring the plans for the new village went rapidly forward and soon pretty little concrete houses with roofs of scarlet and trimmings of green dotted the slopes on the opposite side of the river. The laying out and building of this community became Grandfather Fernald's recreation and delight. Morning, noon, and evening he could be seen either perusing curling sheets of blue prints, consorting with his architects, or rolling off in his car to inspect the progress of the venture. Sometimes he took Ted with him, sometimes his son, and when Laurie was strong enough, the entire family frequently made the pilgrimage to the new settlement.

It was very attractive, there was no denying that; and it seemed as if nothing that could give pleasure to its future residents had been omitted. The tiny library had been Laurie's pet scheme, and not only had his grandfather eagerly carried out the boy's own plans but he had proudly ordered the lad's name to be chiselled across the front of the building. Ted's plea had been for a playground and this request had also been granted, since it appeared to be a wise one. It was a wonderful playground, bordering on the river and having swings and sand boxes for the children; seats for tired mothers; and a large ball-field with bleachers for the men and boys. The inhabitants of Freeman's Falls had never dreamed of such an ideal realm in which to live, and as tidings of the paradise went forth, strangers began to flock into town in the hope of securing work in the mills and homes in the new settlement.

The Fernalds, however, soon made it plain that the preference was to be given to their old employees who had served them well and faithfully for so many years. Therefore, as fast as the houses were completed, they were assigned to those who had been longest in the company's employ and soon the streets of the new village were no longer silent but teemed with life and the laughter of a happy people. And among those for whom a charming little abode was reserved were the Turners, Ted's family.

Then came the tearing down of the temporary bridge of wood and the opening of the beautiful stone structure that arched the stream. Ah, what a holiday that was! The mills were closed, there was a band concert in the little park, dedication exercises, and fireworks in the evening. And great was Ted's surprise when he spied cut in the stone the words "Turner's Bridge!" Near the entrance was a modest bronze tablet stating that the memorial had been constructed in honor of Theodore Turner who, by his forethought in giving warning of the freshet of 1912 had saved the village of Freeman's Falls from inestimable calamity.

How the boy blushed when Mr. Lawrence Fernald mentioned him by name in the dedication speech! And yet he was pleased, too. And how the people cheered; and how proud his father and sisters were! Perhaps, however, the most delighted person of all was Laurie who had been in the secret all along and who now smiled radiantly to see his friend so honored.

"The townspeople may not go to my library," he laughed, "but every one of them will use your bridge. They will have to; they can't help it!"

The thought seemed to amuse him vastly and he always referred to the exquisite granite structure with its triple arch and richly carved piers of stone as *Ted's Bridge.*

Thus did the year with its varied experiences slip by and when June came the Fernalds carried Laurie to New York to consult the much heralded Viennese surgeon. Ah, those were feverish, anxious days, not only for the Fernald family but for Ted and Mr. Hazen as well. The boy and the tutor had remained at Pine Lea there to continue their studies and await the tidings Laurie's father had promised to send them; and when the ominous yellow telegrams with their momentous messages began to arrive, they hardly knew whether to greet them with sorrow or rejoicing.

They need not, however, have dreaded the news for after careful examination the eminent specialist had decided to take a single desperate chance and operate with the hope of success. Laurie, they were told, was a monument of courage and had the spirit of a Spartan. Unquestionably he merited the good luck that followed for fortune did reward his heroism,—smiling fortune. Of course, the miracle of health could not come all in a moment; months of convalescence must follow which would be unavoidably tedious with suffering. But beyond this arid stretch of pain lay the goal of recovery.

No lips could tell what this knowledge meant to those who loved the boy. In time he was to be as strong as any one! It was unbelievable. Nevertheless, the roseate promise was no dream. Laurie was brought home to Pine Lea and immediately the mending process began. Already one could read in the patient face the transformation hope had wrought. There was some day to be college, not alone for Ted but for Laurie himself,—college, and sports, and a career.

In the fullness of time these long-anticipated joys began to arrive. Health made its appearance and at its heels trouped success and happiness; and to balance them came gratitude, humility, and service. In the meantime, with every lengthening year, the friendship between Laurie and Ted toughened in fiber and became a closer bond. And it was not engineering or electricity that ultimately claimed the constructive interest of the two comrades but instead the Fernald mills, which upon Grandfather Fernald's retirement called for younger men at their helm. So after going forth into the great world and whetting the weapons of their intellect they found the dragon they had planned to slay waiting for them at home in Freeman's Falls. Yet notwithstanding its familiar environment, it was a very real dragon and resolutely the two young men attacked it, putting into their management of the extensive industry all the spirit of brotherhood that burned in their hearts and all the desire for service which they cherished. With the aim of bringing about a kindlier coöperation and fuller sympathy between capital and labor they toiled, and the world to which they gave their efforts was the better for it.

Nevertheless, they did not entirely abandon their scientific interests for on the border of the river stood a tiny shack equipped with a powerful wireless apparatus. Here on a leisure afternoon Ted Turner and his comrade could often be found capturing from the atmosphere those magic sounds that spelled the intercourse of peoples, and the thought of nations; and often they spoke of Alexander Graham Bell and those patient pioneers who, together with him, had made it possible for the speech of man to traverse continents and circle a universe.

www.ingramcontent.com/pod-product-compliance
Lightning Source LLC
Chambersburg PA
CBHW061449210726
48287CB00007B/2424